SIGNATURE
ANTHOLOGY

SIGNATURE ANTHOLOGY

by

Samuel Beckett·Elspeth Davie·
Eva Figes·Kenneth Gangemi·
Aidan Higgins·Eugene Ionesco·
Robert Nye·Jan Quackenbush·
Ann Quin·Nicholas Rawson

Calder & Boyars
London

First published in Great Britain in 1975
by Calder and Boyars Limited
18 Brewer Street
London W1R 4AS

© the authors 1975
'How to Cook a Hard Boiled Egg' originally
published as *Comment préparer un œuf dur* by
Editions Gallimard,
Paris 1968
ALL RIGHTS RESERVED

ISBN 0 7145 0970 1

Photosetting by Thomson Press (India) Limited,
New Delhi.
Printed in Great Britain by Whitstable Litho.

CONTENTS

		Page
Samuel Beckett	STILL	11
Elspeth Davie	THE LAST WORD	17
Eva Figes	BEDSITTER and OBLIGATO	31
Kenneth Gangemi	MEXICO—A WORK IN PROGRESS	49
Aidan Higgins	DISTANT FIGURES	69
Eugene Ionesco	HOW TO COOK A HARD BOILED EGG	91
Robert Nye	TRUE THOMAS	97
Jan Quackenbush	SIMEON IN MEMORIUM	109
Ann Quin	EYES THAT WATCH BEHIND THE WIND	131
Nicholas Rawson	JULY'S FOUR	151

INTRODUCTION

This anthology in the *Signature Series* contains short works by ten established writers and varies widely in style and content. Further Anthologies will appear in the future as this appears to be the most satisfactory way of making available, in permanent form, the important shorter work of eminent contemporary writers, which would otherwise only have a short life in magazines.

SAMUEL BECKETT was born in 1906 in Dublin, and is generally recognized as one of the most significant creative minds of this century. Recognition came late, but his circle of readers has rapidly expanded since the great international success of *Waiting for Godot* in 1952. He has since turned out a stream of novels, plays and other work, all deeply pessimistic in their view of the human condition, but containing such startling insights into human behaviour and motivation, so lucid and poetic in style, and with so much warmth and humour, that he has broken through to general public acceptance, even with his shorter and more demanding recent work. He has become an acclaimed and much admired classic in his own time. He was given the Nobel Prize for Literature in 1969. *Still* is a short text, typical of the later quietist Beckett.

7

ELSPETH DAVIE was born, and lives in, Edinburgh. She has published two novels, *Providings* and *Creating A Scene* and her second volume of short stories will appear shortly. Winner of the Observer Short Story Competition in the 1950's she has since appeared in most of the quality literary magazines and her reputation as a unique fiction writer grows steadily. All her work is a very personal view of the duality or the tension between people and the objects or pre-occupations that dominate them. Mrs Davie has won a number of awards from the Scottish Arts Council.

EVA FIGES was born in Berlin in 1934, but has lived in England since childhood. She has written five novels and a sociological treatise, *Patriarchal Attitudes* on male domination of women, as well as publishing a number of translations. She won the Guardian Fiction Prize for her novel *Winter Journey*.

KENNETH GANGEMI was born in 1937 in the United States, where he has been praised as an unusual stylist. His novella *Olt* has been published in Britain, the United States, France and Germany. *Mexico* is part of a work in progress.

AIDAN HIGGINS was born in 1927 and is undoubtedly one of the best-known serious Irish novelists of his age group. He has published two novels, one book of short stories and other writings. He won the James Tait Black Memorial Prize for *Langrishe, Go Down* and was a runner-up for the 1972 Booker Prize with *Balcony of Europe*. His work combines poetic visual imagery with an indirect expression of nostalgia and emotion.

EUGENE IONESCO was born in 1912 in Rumania, but has always lived in France. He has for twenty years been one of the best-known playwrights on the international scene. His work dramatizes the absurdities that he perceives around him in life and in language, but has become increasingly sombre in recent years. An obsession with eggs runs throughout his work and is light-heartedly expressed in *How to Cook a Hard Boiled Egg*.

ROBERT NYE was born in 1939 and lives in Scotland. He is well known as a novelist, poet, playwright and critic and is one of the most highly regarded fiction reviewers of the present time. His novel *Doubtfire* and volume of short stories *Tales I Told My Mother* both express a personal mystique that owes something to medieval preoccupations, and his gift for fantasy is evident in his children's poems and the fable in this volume.

JAN QUACKENBUSH was born in 1944 in Pennsylvania. He has written mostly plays and some prose, much of it recently concerned with his experiences in the Vietnam War. He writes about simple situations, often about children, with a very personal style that tends to be charged with a strong emotional strain but always stops short of sentimentality. His plays have been performed in many countries including Britain.

9

ANN QUIN was born in 1937, and with her first novel, *Berg*, was acclaimed internationally. She received many scholarships and bursaries on the strength of her singular talent. From the macabre semi-naturalism of her first book, her later work became increasingly interior and her last novel, *Tripticks*, was much influenced by jazz-improvisation. She died tragically by drowning in 1973, leaving an irreplaceable gap in British letters.

NICK RAWSON, born in 1934, came to us, like Aidan Higgins, with a recommendation from Samuel Beckett. A poet, who has experimented with many forms, his gift is plainly for the long semi-narrative impression of mood and scene as glimpsed by the distorting lens of consciousness. He is the author of *Shards*, a book-length prose poem.

Samuel Beckett

STILL

STILL

Bright at last close of a dark day the sun shines
out at last and goes down. Sitting quite still at
valley window normally turn head now and see it
the sun low in the southwest sinking. Even get up
certain moods and go stand by western window
quite still watching it sink and then the afterglow.
Always quite still some reason some time past
this hour at open window facing south in small
upright wicker chair with armrests. Eyes stare
out unseeing till first movement some time past
though unseeing still while still light. Quite still
again then all quite quiet apparently till eyes open
again while still light though less. Normally turn
head now ninety degrees to watch sun which if
already gone then fading afterglow. Even get up

certain moods and go stand by western window till quite dark and even some evenings some reason long after. Eyes then open again while still light and close again in what if not quite a single movement almost. Quite still again then at open window facing south over the valley in this wicker chair though actually close inspection not still at all but trembling all over. Close inspection namely detail by detail all over to add up finally to this whole not still at all but trembling all over. But casually in this failing light impression dead still even the hands clearly trembling and the breast faint rise and fall. Legs side by side broken right angles at the knees as in that old statue some old god twanged at sunrise and again at sunset. Trunk likewise dead plumb right up to top of skull seen from behind including nape clear of chairback. Arms likewise broken right angles at the elbows forearms along armrests just right length forearms and rests for hands clenched lightly to rest on ends. So quite still again then all quite quiet apparently eyes closed which to anticipate when they open again if they do in time then dark or some degree of starlight or moonlight or both. Normally watch night fall however long from this narrow chair or standing by western window quite still either case. Quite still namely staring at some one thing alone such as tree or bush a detail alone if near if far the whole if far enough till it goes. Or by eastern window certain moods staring at some point on the hillside such as that beech in whose shade once quite still till it goes. Chair some reason always same place same position facing south as though clamped down whereas in reality no lighter no more movable imaginable. Or anywhere any ope staring out at nothing just failing light quite still till quite dark though of course no such thing just less light still when less did not seem possible. Quite still then all this time eyes open when discovered then closed then opened and closed again no other movement any kind though of course not still at all when suddenly or so it looks this movement impossible to follow let alone describe. The right hand slowly opening leaves the armrest taking with it the whole forearm complete with elbow and slowly rises opening further as it goes and turning a little deasil till midway to the head it hesitates and hangs half open trembling in mid air. Hangs there as if half inclined to return that is sink back slowly closing as it goes and turning the other way till as and where it began clenched lightly on end of rest. Here because of what comes now not midway to the head but almost there before it hesitates and hangs there trembling as if half inclined etc. Half no but on the verge when in its turn the head moves from its place forward and down among the ready fingers where no sooner received and held it weighs on down till elbow meeting armrest brings this last movement to an end and all still once more. Here back a little way to that suspense before head to rescue as if hand's need the greater and on down in what if not quite a single movement almost till elbow against rest. All quite still again then head in hand namely thumb on outer edge of right socket index ditto left and middle on left check-bone plus as the hours pass lesser contacts each more or less now more now less with the faint stirrings of the various parts as night wears on. As if even in the dark eyes closed not enough and perhaps even more than ever necessary against that no such thing the further shelter of the hand. Leave it so all quite still or try listening to the sounds all quite still head in hand listening for a sound.

Elspeth Davie

THE LAST WORD

THE LAST WORD

Very early in life Pirie decided that the world owed him a lot and that never, for as long as he might live, could the debt be made up. But he could still take back something for himself. It was natural for him as a child to take everything that moved under his hand. He went after fluffballs and the twists of paper that fell from pockets. He chased tickets and picked up the feathers dropped by birds. He was like a bird himself. His bead-green eyes scanned the ground as through a magnifying lens. Later he interested himself in scatterings of coins, notes and cigarettes. He was no different in this from any other. But as he grew older he lifted his head from the ground and saw things ready for the taking on shelves and ledges. He hardly needed a conjuror's skill to dip into the fruit baskets of small shops or remove four or five from a row of identical leeks. The world owed him melons as well as plums. It owed him serving-plates as well as ashtrays. But the small things were easiest to stow.

When he was grown and on a level with others his eyes never melted with theirs. His parents seemed to him as smugly respectable as the two white china figures on either side of their wedding-day clock which had been allowed to run slow ever since. Two brothers and a sister had made themselves ridiculous, in his eyes, by passively accepting over the years the uniforms, the wages, the dead-ends of their various jobs. He despised them for this. He was intelligent himself, good both with head and hands. But he had a dread of the static life. Instead he went in and out of an endless variety of trades, helping himself as he left to tools and clocks, towels, lamps and paper-weights. He was on his way to becoming a petty thief, yet the name didn't suit him. He had begun to have judgement. He seldom picked an ugly thing though he took useless ones. Nor was it certain he'd be thrown into ecstasy even if his foot had accidentally grated on a diamond. This might have seemed crude and obvious as a free gift. It would have meant fate had softened towards him and he had no use for softness.

But he had to have money. He'd built up a car-cleaning business with another man. He'd assembled furniture, assisted a firm of auctioneers and tried juggling dishes in restaurant-cars between London and Edinburgh. But at the same time his own liftings became more ambitious. He was no smasher or slasher. He had grown excessively reserved and in certain ways almost as respectable as his family had been. Gradually the pilfering grew into a fine art. To take jobs for money was one thing. This was something else. Nowadays the world didn't owe him anything or everything. It owed him the best, the unusual, the hard-to-get. There were never many things in his room at one time for he was never satisfied. He discarded endlessly, letting go of one prize only to pick a better. A model ship changed places with binoculars which were replaced, after a week or two, by a chessboard, a chunk of agate, a stuffed heron with toes embedded in blue rock. The best was to be had if only he could lay hands on it. When it was found he was willing to pay and pay high, for he was after pearls of price. Meantime he helped himself.

Pirie saw himself as quick, cool and deliberate. But he could look frantic, casting wildly about in case something had escaped him and gnawed by the fear that, for all his skill, he might have put his hand on the second rate when all the time the best was in another town or another country. His things had been got at risk. In every case the taking could not have been more difficult if it had been accompanied by thunderclaps. But he was not after ease. He had an eye for colour, but it was an anguished eye. He brooded on the notion that even colour might have escaped him—not just a shade, but some undiscovered primary colour which he might had missed through defective vision or simply because a human eye had serious limitations.

Pirie professed scorn at limits. But the difficulties of his secret trade had given him one overwhelming obsession. It was the wastefulness of the natural world which mystified and fascinated him. He felt unease at the superabundance, the spill-over of the earth's stuff. At times he felt fury. He had a puritan's fear of waste, and on a smaller scale, would no more have dreamt of going after things which were free for the taking than he would of bending to pick up those objects thrown up with savage lavishness on the shore in one night's storm. He wondered superstitiously what sort of backlash might come from a force which produced seeds, stars, animals and insects on this colossal scale. There were split seconds when, against such a background, he saw himself as mean to the point of deformity; flashes when, to his own eyes, he appeared bent double as though the furtive minutes of his life had been locked together in one permanent arthritic stoop. This malignant image would fade from his mind as quickly as it had come.

He made discoveries in his own field. Lately he had found he could slice the costly leatherback from the end of a library shelf as neatly as he'd long ago lifted the folded napkins in a hotel lounge. He glanced into these books before he sold them— learnt scraps of old medicine and botany, bored himself blind over theological arguments which might once have startled his great grandfather. There were things in his head which scholars in the subject had missed. He amused himself—but not for long—with travellers' tales, allowed himself to skim momentarily along the blue edges of icebergs or up tropical rivers against a steamy broth of

22

fishes and strange vegetation. What he could not abide was fiction in any form. He knew it for what it was. Lies. He rifled through the classics, through new novels. Columns of conversation caught his eye. He frowned to see the characters turning themselves inside out and upside down to one another's view. He scanned a volume from first page to last to find one mention of the hero's job and was scandalized to reach the end no better informed. He jumped passages of love-making as across raging torrents, landing pages on in a new crowd, a new city, and immediately taking off again, skimming, jumping till he found a last landing-place on which to take his stand. And his standpoint never changed. There was nothing here for him, and there was nothing because it was lies, all lies from start to finish.

About this time he discovered one day on the outskirts of the city a secondhand bookshop which he hadn't known of before. It was not a place for rich bindings. While he hung about for a few minutes he accidentally knocked a pile of magazines from a stool and was setting them up again when the owner spoke from the back of the shop.

"Take them! Take the lot. You can have them for thirty pence."

It seemed more a gift than a bargain.

"Thanks, no," said Pirie, starting to pile them again.

"What!" said the man.

"I don't want them." Pirie spoke coldly, scarcely moving his lips. But he bent and picked a magazine off the pile, then slowly another, and another. It was a periodical on Astronomy and each number had a coloured cover. On one was a whirlpooling, greenish galaxy, hurling off stars, on another a globular cluster dense at its centre as a snowball; on another a blacked-out sun in eclipse, the corona frayed with scarlet loops and spirals; on another a blue nebula veil. Twelve in all. And on the last, set against black space, were the minute, tilted discs of distant galaxies. Pirie's heart had jumped at these sights. His shoulders remained rigid as he flipped them through.

"A good set," said the man watching him and flicking his duster over a table of books. "A bit tattered. But the photos are magnificent."

"I don't need them." Pirie's voice was pitched thin and high.

"The photos *and* the text. Both excellent. The text is a bit out of date. That's the only reason they're going cheap. That and a few stains here and there."

"Out of date?" Pirie turned his head and spoke with contempt. But it was for his own eagerness he felt the greatest scorn.

"By out of date," said the man evenly, "I mean not much more than fifteen years or so. But I'll admit a few years can bring out a hell of a lot of new kinks in the cosmos. Another ten might show the whole affair turned inside out. But look at your pictures! Will you ever see better?"

Pirie gathered up the journals awkwardly, dropped a couple, gathered them up again and tried to pile them on the stool.

"Yes, that's how it is," said the man coming forward. "They'll clutter the place up, getting more tattered at every move. Twenty pence then. Take them or leave them." As though conferring a particular favour Pirie took them.

For the rest of that day and well on into the night he went through the magazines. He sat first at his table, then at the fire, and finally on the floor, back to the wall. Once or twice he lay and stared up as though to pierce the plaster with his eyes. He had known about stars. He had made it his business years ago. But this lot burst without warning through everything he'd known before. Certain ideas had been blown to smithereens. With each page he turned the limits exploded further and further out. On the digits which stood for time and space the O's were multiplying like pond eggs in the sun.

Faced again with a shattering of confines Pirie reacted with the usual exhilaration and dread. But it went deeper than before. Next day, surrounded by magazines, he ate and drank with stars. He stirred his tea on the verge of spinning galaxies and noted how stars and liquid swirled together. He explored vast outpourings and sank through appalling extinctions, brooded on the blazing growth of super giants which had collapsed into dense seeds. While he finished supper he found in the last number of the pile, one page uncut. He slit it quickly with the breadknife and a great, blunt-nosed comet whizzed into view. He stopped eating and brooded superstitiously on the comet. Why *he* the first to see it? He turned back to earlier numbers and went slowly on with his meal, stopping now and then to read or hold a page up to examine the almost invisible double of a star.

And the day after he went through the pile again. By this time he'd got a grip on himself, cooled to the point of calm. After a week he was in control and his final conclusion was that once again he'd been sold short, and with only himself to blame. For he remembered he'd been warned. This was out of date information, tattered facts. He brooded over it for a day or two as he went about doing other jobs, and finally he could hardly bring himself to glance at the magazines. In their way they were now no better than fiction. They were not completely true and that was the end of it. Each day they grew more tattered as though his angry eyes were reducing them to trash, and at last came the day when they were tied and dumped outside in the waste-paper sack. He missed the turbulence and luminosity of the photos more than he'd thought possible. He was out of a whirlpool, and the ground he was on felt deadly flat. But he was no child, he said, to be placated with pictures if the rest was wrong.

Yet his mind ran more than ever on stars. One day, not many weeks after he'd dumped the magazines, he spotted a book on Astronomy in the main bookshop of the city. The huge volume, heavy as a tablet of stone, had everything. Amongst the 900 pages of text were coloured photos as good and better than any he'd seen, diagrams and drawings by masters, with maps of the sky folded between the front and back covers. The book was written by experts and recommended by experts. It was full of the poetry and the mathematics of stars, and it was fresh from the publisher. Pirie knew what he'd found. There could be no question of making a grab for it. Bargaining was out. This was the pearl, and he would pay for it. He examined the £12 price ticket. He examined the publication date again to make sure of year and month, checked the corners of the book to see that it was perfect and rifled quickly through in case anyone had left a print on the new pages. There was no flaw in it. Finally he opened the book in the centre and sniffed. The print smelt bitter and fresh at the same time. To Pirie it smelt of the blackness of outer space, but space confined. And now owned. For by a stroke of luck he had money enough in his pockets. He walked to the desk with the book under his arm and began to leaf out the seven single pounds and the five pound note. This he did with some arrogance, sharply rapping the side of his thumb down on top of each note as he flipped it out as though each one, for the benefit of un-believers, must be both seen and heard. There was a slight altercation over wrapping.

"It would be better to have it wrapped," said the assistant.

"I'll take it as it is."

"It is customary for books to leave our premises wrapped."

"I'll take it as it is or not at all."

The assistant nodded. Pirie left the desk with his unwrapped book under his arm, and he took his time. There were a few people around. Nearby a fat man who was leaning against a shelf of cookery books, reading recipes, smiled at Pirie as he went past. Pirie had made no study of smiles and had no clue to the meaning of this one. He paused, took the book from under his arm and ceremoniously unfolded the black and white star-map at the back, letting it hang over his elbow almost to the ground while he studied it. The fat man detached himself from the shelf. "That's some book you've got there!" he murmured to the bent head. There was no response. Pirie had risked himself more than most but he had an instinct that the spontaneous word, friendly or hostile, might one day destroy him. The man took a couple of steps forward till he stood at Pirie's elbow. "It seems we've a common interest," he said. "And that *is* a book! *That* one's a prize!" He touched the ruffled stream of stars with one finger.

"Yes!" said Pirie sharply.

"And you've wasted no time at all. It's as crisp from the press as a cake from the oven."

"Yes!" Pirie quickly folded the map and closed the book. "It's the last word."

"The latest. O, of course!" said the fat man. "Right up to the mark. *Not*, naturally, the last word."

Pirie's heart jerked. He sensed a threat. He felt his limits strain and snap. "The last word!" he said again, drawing his breath in sharply.

"We can't fool ourselves, can we?" said the fat man smiling. "There *is* no last word. Can't be and never will be."

Pirie was moving away but he turned his head to throw a cold, galled glare behind. "Till next year then—the last word!" he said.

"Get along—you're joking!" the other replied. "Not till next month or next week or tomorrow. The last word? Not even till the next split second!"

Pirie had reached the door but he turned again.

28

"What do you think I paid for?" he asked in his cold, clipped voice.

"To be always on the move—and in the dark," said the fat man genially as Pirie stepped outside and started off down the street. "To be aghast—endlessly!" he called after him. He stood for a minute watching Pirie, then came softly back and took up his stance at the shelf. Pirie was already two blocks away. On one side of him moved lines of cars. On the other, a jostling crowd. Shadows of chimneys, of awnings, trees and lamp-posts moved on the ground in front and behind. But these were not the only movements conspiring to unfix him. There was a vibration of dust and light in the air, an endless drift of light and dark particles circling alone or in groups—so erratic, so devious, there was no knowing whether they belonged to his own eyes, to the outside world, or to both. Moving rapidly, but with the painful precision of a tightroper slung in the void, Pirie went along the uneven edges of the pavement, his eyes down.

Eva Figes

BEDSITTER
and
OBLIGATO

BEDSITTER

Electricity twenty, no that's not accurate, much more in the winter, how long till winter, nine months, ages away, rent due at the end of the month that makes another twenty, dear god and I'm running through cash at the rate of fifteen a week, must stop smoking cut down on alcohol where did I put the matches where was I, yes, as I was saying the important thing is to concentrate on work, produce, thrust forward, never mind about trivialities, that's what fools some, little minds, who cares about tomorrow, newspapers, ought to pick up old ones instead of buying, what's the good of reading that trash anyhow, all the same, a decision has to be made, if I sold those books, and I've not worked, how long now, two days?

Three? And when I was, what good was it, those months? Must decide, can't just stay put, do nothing, perhaps I could stop eating, waste away to nothing, one solution, afterwards, what would they do, throw the body out at the back with unwanted bits of lumber, or perhaps so emaciated, so long for someone to knock, I would have vanished altogether, that would be a laugh, the old girl not able to demand her arrears, like to see her face.

This is no use, not facing up to it. Sat down, remember, biro and a scrap of paper, to work it out in figures, only each time I back away before I begin, because you don't have to go far to see that brick wall staring you in the face. Outgoings: food five rent five heating two lighting god knows smokes four lighting paper books laundry shit shoe leather reading matter conversation and ultimately escape. All have to be paid for. Income nil. Simple really, use the scrap of paper to wipe your arse.

So: time is running out, always was, think about work only work, that's the important thing, never mind about anything else, all you have got, a few hours, years perhaps, don't look back or down, lose your balance and fall off, don't let them distract you, the rats, rat race, show what's inside, reveal to an astonished world, and they will be astonished, amazed, I promise you, I will do such things, what was the quotation, words float in a black void, like debris in outer space, I will do such things, actor's voice full of power and passion echoing in a black hollow space, proscenium arch, rehearsal, only what was the play called?

God my stomach, killing me, it's my nerves I know that, eating irregularly, give it up altogether, perhaps I should go to bed, must be getting late, stop this pacing about, smoking does no good, nearly out anyhow, have to go to the machine, it'll be the death of you, poor father, always going on about his health, my health rather, a young chap like you with a long way to go, gave up smoking, drinking, everything, all regulated, much good it did him, caught him anyhow, and now I've wasted his savings, thirty years in the same job, putting a bit by year in year out, blown it all in what, less than ten months I make it, he would not have approved, definitely not, too bad I was his only son, no one else to leave it to, it's time father I shouted at him, so excited I really was shouting, all I want is time to do what I want, that's what I told him one of the few times I took the trouble to go down and see him, poor old chap, if I'd realized perhaps I'd have gone down a bit more, how was I to know, always so satisfied, not a day off sick in near on ten years, used to boast about it.

Was it wasted, that's what I don't know, floating about like an astronaut who has lost his bearings, thinking it's all bad bad bad, am I right way up, upside down, nobody to judge, talk to.

What I should really do is buy a telescope and put it on the roof. I could spend hours up there on clear nights, climb up through the skylight.

Space being infinite since stars must continue for always in time and space which cannot come to a stop it follows with sure mathematical certainty that life must also be repeated an infinite number of times. Since it does not matter how small the chance, pick any number, one in nine, nine million, in relation to infinity it makes little or no odds, no matter how small, or large, the chance of gas exploding, matter cooling to manageable life proportions of oxygen, carbon, sea and land, and since each star lives in its own blackness of which we are totally ignorant the chances may be much higher than arrogance allows us to suppose, but even if small, so small, with stars being infinite it is still large enough for life, the world as we know it, to be repeated in its various stages ad infinitum. So the universe is its own eternity, ours too, if it matters.

Imagine, out in the black all round a man the identical replica of my father is not only dying, moving, but being born, blinking into a first light which will reach here long after we are burnt out and black. If I was to study the night sky through a telescope I would be looking into distant million light years away. But our own star will not blink until it is dead, exists in the future. Past, future, all done with mirrors, ding dong.

I can hear the old girl moving about, perhaps she is going to come up and complain, like last night, about the noise I made in the night pacing up and down, is it my fault if I can't sleep, god knows I wish I could, the floorboards are terrible, really mister er, never sure what to call me, I suppose I do have a name, I can feel the furniture shake with every foot you put down, this is an old house and so am I, and I really will have to ask you to leave at the end of the month if you can't lie down after midnight the way other people do.

36

And, she added pointedly, other people have jobs to go to, can't afford to sleep all day.

I suppose I could go back, cap in hand, and ask for my old job back. Could I stand it, bear it, those faces, imposed procedures, catch the bus winter mornings, summer, dark in the winter, cold, sharp at eight thirty to be in at nine, late of course, everyone sliding backwards to avoid, what? Something. You give up what you are, all you can do is cheat, stare out of the window and watch clouds form above rooftops, doodle shapes on company paper, steal company time by coming in ten minutes late, because you know the other chap is always twelve minutes late. Could I, would they have me now, is it too late, a self-avowed crank, suppose I told them I had solved the mystery of the universe, so simple, how come no one has ever thought of it before, how could someone who catches buses, how could anyone who does not dare to lose his bearings, and I have, once you understand about black, matter floating in space, would say I was mad, and am of course, life which is consciousness should not become aware, realize itself from the outside, living organisms are a blind circuit, once realize that and the circuit is broken, what is the point, none, so that paralysis must follow, contemplate the mathematical proof of eternity in an age when it comes too late to mean anything, matter that has no meaning, that is only itself.

The old girl has gone back down without stopping on my landing, or knocking at the door. Pity, could have told, tried it out on her, must have been a girl once, still inside, that was the worst of it, girls laughing, smoothly combed hair, wasting cash on cinema for two, falsely inviting smile painted on sliding imperceptibly into awful laughter. Perhaps she has gone to another job, or married.

Do not want to go back, on the other hand, does not add up, cannot live on promises, uncommercial, that's the best I've heard, what they all say, of course not, how can you commercialize losing one's bearings, whirling in space, not able or willing to go back to the old circuit, I must just lie here, high perhaps, tuned in to my own internal telescope, spying into the dark future and the bright past, like a star dying, what is left of my body burning itself up, no need for food or for what cash could buy. That is what I shall do. And like a star, when someone finds me, I shall have gone.

OBLIGATO

and then there's the floors when did I last do the
landing only yesterday yes yesterday afternoon
and just look at it now just a waste of time why
can't they be a bit more careful I keep nagging
till I'm sick of hearing my own voice doing it and
none of it makes the slightest bit of difference I
might just as well save my breath and perhaps if
I did we'd all get on a bit better just let everything
go why not let the mess pile up see how they like
it then no meals on time the beds not made they're
old enough to make their own and then new sheets
they look a sight Peggy has a tear in her top one
says her foot keeps going through it making it
bigger of course instead of mending it herself
can't even put a button back on her overcoat

39

though she's fond enough of sewing when it comes to make something new a useless toy but then they never think is it any wonder I get irritable I could just about throw something though what good would that do they've started calling me an old cow bitch things like that and I suppose it must look like it to them just like their father is always telling them and you can't expect them to understand they haven't been through it not yet their turn will come poor little sods I suppose it'll have to be brussels sprouts again such a fiddle half of them frostbitten not worth tenpence a pound really paying double when most of them get thrown away and the work still labour-saving things always cost more money and beggars can't be choosers and if it had been left to him there'd have been nothing on the table at all for the past four months I mean you can't live on air and a lot of promises while they take little holidays trips to the seaside and so on that's what makes me so angry but of course they don't see that if I'd bought leeks this week it would have worked out cheaper still it'll have to do now hardly anything left to boil not that I'm hungry the smell of that roast cooking turns me over not myself this morning all my insides feel as though they were jammed up together period isn't due yet can't be that one mercy anyhow kept out of trouble these past few years got good at it if I'd know then what I know now I need never have got married in the first place still that's all past and done with I hope they're hungry I can't eat a thing today if I could just once say let's get out of this dump and eat in style no preparations no washing up I expect then I'd quite enjoy it work up an appetite after all but it costs too much you know that use your common sense nobody else ever has but for all the thanks you get might as well give up once and for all these four walls these bloody four walls washing them down won't do any good they need painting a man about the house but I'd like to see his face if I asked him probably never show up again probably never will again anyhow hasn't rung for five days that's what's really eating you isn't it all the time you're waiting for the telephone to ring and shouting at the kids as though it were their fault don't think about it doesn't make it any better perhaps I could paint the kitchen myself one evening should do it after they've gone to bed nothing better to do only by then I just want to fall into bed myself you know how you feel no energy left perhaps watch something on the television too tired to switch it off a tonic that's what you need something to buck you up give over you know you're just depressed fed up with everything could cry if it weren't for the kids have to keep up a front with them around mustn't let them see that you're suffering if I could only get them out of the way crawl into a hole and never come out again that's the trouble you always have to come out again and they'll be back wanting another meal put a good front on it pretend nothing has happened nothing is happening after all mothers don't have a right to feelings of their own they just exist to clean up afterwards I know he's gone for good got himself a new woman someone younger no kids ties always in the way still awake when he wants it all the bother of getting Mrs. Lyons in to babysit only wants a quick lay somewhere to put his prick have it off one pair of legs is as good as another not as good getting flabby wonder if he notices varicose veins but not all that bad not in a dim light next year I'll be thirty-nine not even a proper evening out planned with a real show dressed smart just steak and chips if we're eating drinks at the local a film if he's in the mood his mood of course I'm not consulted and in two years I'll be forty then who'll look at me no one not with all this work and being on my feet all day that's what puts years on you so that's it isn't it can't afford to be choosy get on your high horse and the worst of it is

DINNER'S ON THE TABLE

with this one I thought I really thought more fool you he's different warm-hearted my type in a way I don't know what it was but I felt right away we could be good friends companionship about the same age both been through a lot he understands nothing romantic not necessarily well a bit of that too perhaps after all why not we're all young at heart

I SAID DINNER'S ON THE TABLE. CAN'T YOU COME WHEN YOU'RE CALLED

and if it's going to be ever it's got to be now time's running out and I really felt all those years that nothing would ever happen it had all been a fraud a put up job you get tricked into hoping and that's what keeps you going going on somehow but when he came along I thought well perhaps I was right and I got that lifting feel under my ribs perhaps I was right to keep on waiting not cheapen myself you know any port in a storm

YOU EAT IT AND LIKE IT. BELT UP
I was right all along we understand each other
I feel safe with him someone you can really lean on
a bit not just out for what he can get a selfish bastard
like their father

HE'D HAVE LEFT YOU TO THE COUN-
CIL. JUST REMEMBER THAT

try getting him to look after you day in day out and
see how you like it what happens ungrateful little
bastards left it all to me you slave for them day
after day and the moment you think they're getting
old enough to appreciate all you've done what
you're doing they turn round and start criticizing
quoting their father at you he's got a nerve talking
to them like that after walking out on them they
don't remember that of course and I don't suppose
he's got round to mentioning it walking out with
that piece barely nineteen the rent wasn't even paid
and not a penny in the house the coal bunker empty
and nearly Christmas I notice she isn't too keen to
start a family oh no but she'll feel the pinch too
when the judge hears about it and he will I'll see to
that he says he'll see about legal aid it just takes time
months and months what are you supposed to
live on in the meantime you tell me that nobody
does of course perhaps I should let them cut the
telephone off that would save a bit for all the good
it does me dear god if he gives them a bob each on
Saturday and tells them to go and buy a lollipop
they think he's god and those roller skates they'll
kill themselves on those roller skates but of course
he doesn't think of that I'm just a nagging old
woman

43

So can we?
WHAT?
Haven't been listening. Can we go out?
IT'S RAINING
But yesterday you said
YESTERDAY I DIDN'T KNOW IT WAS
GOING TO RAIN TODAY DID I? NOW
LEAVE ME ALONE

if only they would but then it's raining and where
else is there to go they get irritable just like me
cooped up all day I suppose I should be more
patient make allowances they don't understand
how I feel how can they not only feel but look an
absolute sight hair not done for a week no wonder
he doesn't want to know isn't interested just a
nagging old woman they're quite right their father
is too I suppose I must have given them hell
sometimes getting into a state like this all I want
to do is shout yell at them litter all over the table if I
could take time not just wash my hair have a long
hot bath clean clothes from top to toe not just clean
have to be new slam the door go somewhere where
that's the point don't have the face to start off by
myself no courage is there any point and there's
no question of a new coat perhaps I could turn the
hem or put a bit of fur round the collar that might
look quite nice set off my face since the television
keeps making crackling noises and if it goes I shall
get no peace from them at all apart from which that
stair carpet is getting really dangerous that's twice
I've caught my heel on it and nearly gone head first
and if one of them had an accident I should never
forgive myself perhaps if I paid something down
telephone the phone is ringing quick now sound

casual what's the difference anyhow one day more or less another wrong number another wrong bloody number am I the Odeon cinema what the hell what the hell did you expect

GIVE HIM HIS BALL BACK. STOP QUARRELLING

can't they stop rowing for one minute men are all the same what did you expect aren't you ever going to learn learn any sense at your time of life in a minute I shall belt both of them I don't care who started it enough to drive one mad can't they keep quiet for one minute dear god I don't know what I shall do but very soon I shall do something something I'll be sorry for later when I've had a chance to cool down

I've hurt my knee

SERVES YOU RIGHT

and it does too if I've told him once I've told him a dozen times not to play on those back steps anyway it's not serious just a scratch won't do him any harm not to be fussed over all the time they've got to learn sooner or later might as well know I'm human too apt to lose my temper though why do I get so irritable anyone would think I didn't love them hated them could kill them yet these are the children I held in my arms when they were small so helpless kept me awake at night the smell of warm milk burped up on the wool blanket the long broken nights choosing names for them getting them weighed once a week innoculated

I'm hungry

SHOULD HAVE EATEN YOUR LUNCH NOW GET OUT WHILE I WASH THIS FLOOR feel a wreck just about done in ready to cry into the bucket never thought when I looked at mum always so bad-tempered looking such a sight in the same filthy old apron always nagging never time for jokes or things like that I used to say mum for pete's sake get yourself a hairdo maybe a new outfit even such a spoil sport what with I should like to know and of course I hadn't any money wasn't working then such a spoil sport when Ted and I felt like a giggle happy like

STOP THAT NOISE

I mean we were only kids natural high spirits but her a wet blanket couldn't take a joke nothing much to choose between us now if you come to think of it that's what I keep telling myself I mean was I happy then I suppose I must have been nineteen and nothing ever shook me for long there was always another day and a new day meant a fresh start hope not like now when you know nothing is ever going to be any different only get worse all it can do when they finally leave here they'll probably hate me all I do is shout at them so how can I expect them not to shout at me shout back it's only natural

NO

all I ever say is no perhaps I should stop it stop myself not bother any more perhaps there's nothing to bother about feel better if I had a good cry he'll have gone off to the club by now no point in listening for the phone

I SAID NO

perhaps I could leave upstairs till tomorrow what's one day's dirt more or less take them out somewhere doesn't even remember their birthdays getting on for forty what can you expect even forgets their names sometimes still I suppose he'll ring when it suits him when he has to have it off who are you to be choosy take offence if he's getting it cheap at the price

Kenneth Gangemi

MEXICO
A Work in Progress

MEXICO

Azotea

In the cities of the United States the rooftops of apartment buildings are generally unused. But in Mexico City the rooftops are considered to be valuable space and are used for many purposes. Thousands of people, mostly students at the university, live on the rooftops in little cubicles called *azoteas*. I first learned about them when I was looking for a place to live—a furnished room or a small apartment. I remember that I would read the *anuncios* in the Mexico City newspapers every morning. I would clip the likely prospects, arrange the clipped ads in geographical order, and then tape them to cards. It was a difficult search. I was competing with thousands of Mexicans who knew Spanish well, who knew Mexico City, who had friends and relatives. One morning I spotted this ad: *Magnifica, amueblada, azotea, señor solo, honorable.* I liked the location, the rent was reasonable, and so I hurried right over. It was *beautiful!* It was just right for me. It was completely furnished with a bed, a desk, and bookshelves. I paid a month's rent to the Señora, took my key and receipt, and spent the next hour on the sunny rooftop, admiring my new *azotea.* I was very happy. In all directions there were fine views of Mexico City. The rooftop also had a cat, a small garden, a pen of rabbits, a few chickens running about, and many pots of flowers. I lived there for three months.

Bakery

When I lived in the village I would walk to the *panadería* every morning to buy hot rolls for breakfast. It was one of my great pleasures. It was still cool at that hour and I would keep in the sun. I remember the cobblestones, the cool morning air, the white walls in bright sunlight. At the bakery I would wait in back of a crowd of women and girls. They would be talking quietly in Spanish. I was usually the only man, and some of them turned their heads and simpered and giggled at my presence. When the rolls came from the oven I liked to watch them press together towards the front: the warm females, clothed in soft cottons, pressing breasts against backs and bellies against buttocks.

Bicycle

In Mexico City I was run over by a bicycle. It was a rainy afternoon and I was crossing the street to the bus stop. Bam! The next thing I knew I was flat on my back in the street. There was no pain, just surprise. You never see the one that hits you. I got up and untangled a fourteen-year-old boy from his bicycle. He began to cry softly. I think he had a sprained or broken ankle. I needed help, but the six people waiting at the bus stop did nothing. They just looked at us with those deadpan Mexican expressions.

Casa

In a Mexican village, a house often appears as a wall facing the street with a door in it. The visitor to Mexico soon learns that everything is behind these walls. Seen from the outside, the *casa* is all defense: the rough masonry walls, the iron bars over the windows, the heavy door facing the street. But inside a man may be quietly reading in a lovely patio, filled with plants and flowers, exposed to the sky and the weather. When I lived in the village I came to identify with the *casa* furnished in the Mexican colonial style. It suited my ascetic temperament. There was no heating system. It was always cool, and sweaters were usually worn. I remember the white walls, the black-painted metal, the inexpensive materials, the stone floors with no rugs, the durable furniture of heavy wood. I felt very much at home in those quiet, sparsely-furnished rooms. There was a good feeling of simplicity, restraint, and permanency.

Domingo

When I lived in the village I had a weekly ritual. I would take a break from my work on Sunday mornings and go to sit in the plaza. The parish church faced on the plaza, and I would wait for the eleven o'clock mass to let out. A few minutes before noon the church bells would start to ring, the wooden doors would swing open, and the people would pour out and begin to cluster in front of the church. I would get up and mingle with them. I remember the scene well: everyone dressed in their best clothes, all the generations mingling, everyone talking, the old people watching their grandchildren, formal introductions and presentations on all sides, much laughter, the young people eyeing each other, the little girls with their hair brushed and shining. It lasted for about ten minutes. I would move about, listening to the voices speaking Spanish, looking at the various people, just responding to it all. It always put me into a fine mood. Once I innocently asked a little boy why all this was happening. He looked at me and said *"Porque es Domingo."*

Eduardo

In Mexico City I knew a twelve-year-old boy named Eduardo. He lived in the next building, and whenever he saw me on the street he would ask me to help him with his English. We would go up to his family's apartment, sit in the living room, and he would practice speaking English with me. I remember that he often confused *chicken* with *kitchen* and *hungry* with *angry*. Eduardo had a large family that included a beautiful fifteen-year-old sister, and I would wait for her to appear. I often hinted to Eduardo that perhaps she would like to practice her English also. But Eduardo jealously guarded me and would not let any of his brothers and sisters come near us. I was *his* American friend. I liked Eduardo very much. He was shy and polite. When I brought him children's books in English from the library he would be very happy. Eduardo had eleven brothers and sisters, and once I made a list of the names and ages of all the children in the family. There was Maria Elena (23), Lourdes (22, married), Pilar (21, married), Cecelia (18), Antonio (17), Virginia (15, the one I liked), Eduardo (12), Gabriela (11), Guillermo (9), Guadalupe (8), Beatriz (4), and Elsa (5 months).

Guadalupe and Asunción

When I lived in the village I studied Spanish for about an hour a day. But it was not enough to simply study Spanish: I needed practice in speaking it. I found that the best way, and the most enjoyable, was to make friends with the various shopgirls of the village and have conversations in Spanish with them. I had already discovered that for some reason I understood women better

55

than men. Most of the shopgirls were teenagers, but a few were in their twenties. Some were very pretty. They were all still single. The girls were always available, and they had little else to do. They often would be leaning in the doorways of their shops, arms folded, looking slightly bored, watching the slow-paced activity of the village. I often wondered what they thought about—probably movies, clothes, cosmetics, their *novios,* romantic daydreams, things to eat, the *serenata* on Sunday, their families and girlfriends, fiestas that were coming up. I remember that on Saturday they were often happy, probably because they were looking forward to Sunday, which is the big day in the Mexican week. It was depressing to think of the cloistered lives ahead of them after marriage. They were all martyrs-to-be. They would have children, begin to put on weight, and become restricted to their home and family. When I knew them, however, they were still slim and single. I remember that my favourites were two attractive girls, bright-eyed and intelligent, who worked in the *Libreria* after school. Their names were Guadalupe and Asunción, and they were seventeen and sixteen. They used the familiar form with me right from the beginning—it was so good to hear that *tu*—and we quickly became friends. Guadalupe and Asunción spoke slowly and clearly, and always corrected my Spanish when I made a mistake. They took pains to teach me the idiomatic expressions. Some people have a special skill in being able to converse with those who do not know their language well, and Guadalupe and Asunción both had it. Not many people in the village bought books, so they always had plenty of time for me. I spent many an afternoon talking with them. It was great fun. I remember that we always took turns buying the three bottles of Mexican soda pop. It was a ritual.

Huaraches

There are different styles of *huaraches*, the Mexican sandals, in almost every region of Mexico. It seems that the higher the elevation, the heavier they are. At the time I lived in Mexico the best *huaraches* for use back in the United States came from Mazatlán. They were thin-soled, light-weight, and quite comfortable. But it is not so easy for many American men to buy *huaraches*. The Mexicans have smaller feet, and it is difficult to find the larger sizes, so usually you must have them made to order. I remember the workshop in Mazatlán where I had my *huaraches* made. There was an old man, who was the owner, and two young men, who were his sons. On two pieces of paper I made pencilled outlines of my feet. I gave them to one of the sons and watched him begin to work. He worked rapidly and skilfully, and it was a pleasure to watch him. I love to observe a skilled craftsman. The radio was playing popular music all the time. There was much laughing and joking among the men and the people who came into the workshop. I was glad that I was able to watch the making of the *huaraches* from begin-ning to end. After I tried them out—they squeek when they are new—and paid for them, I had a little talk with the old man. We discussed the prices of cowhides!

Invisible

When I lived in the village I liked to walk around the market at night. It was dark and they could not see that I was an American. I could observe undetected. I would often buy a *taco de carnita* at a curbside stand and then go sit in a doorway to eat. My clothing was dark and inconspicuous. I would blend into the shadows. After I finished my taco I would sit and watch the passing people. There was usually much activity: they would be setting up for the next day. I would be completely unnoticed. No one expected to see an American sitting in a doorway.

Learned

I was twenty-four when I went to live in Mexico. The time I spent there was a strong influence, but it was only years afterwards that I could begin to truly evaluate the experience. I see now that it changed me and that I learned a great deal. It was in Mexico that I stopped wearing a watch. My concept of time had changed, and a watch became unnecessary. From the Mexicans I also learned not to rush. I learned how to sit quietly in a plaza and be content and do absolutely nothing. That was no small accomplishment for someone who grew up in a success-oriented suburb, devoted to producing contestants for the rat race. I also learned about poverty in Mexico. It was an important part of my education, and it gave me a lasting distaste for bourgeois comforts. I observed how the Mexicans lived, how they survived on low incomes. After seeing that most Mexicans ate tortillas and beans three times a day, my own food requirements were considerably modified. It was all useful information. It came in handy during the years of voluntary poverty back in the United States.

Machete

One of the secrets of travelling on a motorcycle is to take frequent breaks. After an hour or so under the hot Mexican sun, it is a great pleasure. I would often sit in the shade outside a grocery store and drink a cold bottle of Mexican soda pop. I remember an incident that occurred in a small village in Guerrero, when I was taking just such a break on a motorcycle trip. There was a sullen-eyed man with a machete who stopped walking and glared at me. He had just come in from the fields and was hot and dirty. I was sitting in the shade, drinking a bottle of that Mexican soda pop called *Chapparita*. He just stood there and glared at me. I still remember his sweating face. I sometimes think of him— the man with the machete—whenever I read about American imperialism in Latin America.

Mechanic

Once I had a motorcycle breakdown in the middle of nowhere. I was on my way to the Yucatán and was a long way from a source of motorcycle parts. The Mexican mechanic that I found was a young man named Héctor. He missed dinner with the family of his *novia* in order to look at my bike. I remember standing over his shoulder and watching him take my engine apart. He worked rapidly and skilfully, and I began to have confidence in him. Finally he said to my relief that the little bearings were causing the noise: the *chicos*, not the *grandes*. It turned out that the nearest bearings were in Mexico City, 350 miles to the north, but this did not bother Héctor. Like most Mexican mechanics he was skilled at adapting parts and improvising repairs. He began to speak casually of taking off a few thousandths here, a few thousandths there. It would be a big job. In the end he decided to take 55/1000 off the connecting rod and put in oversize bearings. When he said that, I remember thinking: *I hope he knows what he is doing*. But it turned out to be all right. I eventually put another 7500 miles on the motorcycle and never had any more bearing trouble.

Miscellaneous A

Mechanics working on a broken-down bus.... Mexican shopgirls leaning in doorways.... The green-glaze pottery from Michoacán.... Bright sunlight on white walls.... The pat-pat-pat sound of tortillas being made.... The calendars hanging on the walls of Mexican cafes.... A sixteen-year-old Indian girl nursing a baby.... The sad-faced shopkeepers.... Fat priests and skinny children...

The shining black hair of the girls....Fresh-squeezed orange juice at sidewalk stands....The parades of schoolchildren on fiesta days....A pet ocelot walking about a house furnished in Mexican colonial....Girls waiting in line outside a *tortil-lería*....The smell of the exhausts of ancient buses....Gardens and patios hidden behind walls ....Pretty girls walking besides their formidable mothers....The streetcar in Vera Cruz that runs to the beach....Guadalajara on Sunday morning.

Plaza

One of the most attractive aspects of a Mexican town is the public plaza at the centre. I spent many hours sitting in various plazas when I lived in Mexico. It was one of my favourite activities. I would sit quietly, calm and happy and content, looking at the sky and the trees and the passing people. I remember thinking about the wisdom of those who drafted the Spanish laws for the establishment of towns, who knew that they should be centred around a public plaza. I considered it an achievement, for someone with my background, to be able to sit quietly in a plaza and do absolutely nothing. When I lived in Mexico I had the time for such worthwhile activities. Sitting in the plaza I had the time to think about the really important things, such as the differences between morning sunshine and afternoon sunshine. I would often stay long enough in the plaza to observe the movement of the shadows. Sometimes I stayed long enough to perceive the temperature drop as the sun became lower in the sky.

Portales

Some of the provincial cities in Mexico, such as Celaya, Oaxaca, and Morelia, have *portales* that face on the public plaza. These are shaded arcade-like walkways that at certain times are busy with activity. The cafes located under the *portales* put out tables and chairs, and it is often a very pleasant place. I liked to sit at one of the tables and drink *café con leche* and observe the activity. The early evening was my favourite time. Most of the other tables would be occupied by middle-class men in coats and ties. They would be drinking coffee, playing board games, and talking among themselves. I overheard many of the conversations. They tirelessly discussed the subjects that men in provincial cities always discuss.

Second-Class Buses

The great majority of Mexicans own no automobile and travel by second-class bus. There are hundreds of independent companies that operate buses all over Mexico, regularly travelling into even the most remote villages. The buses are quite cheap and relatively efficient. The low cost in pennies-per-mile makes it one of the most inexpensive ways to travel in the world. Breakdowns are common, but the Mexican mechanics are skilled at adapting parts and improvising repairs, and somehow they keep the buses running. When I lived in Mexico I rode the second-class buses many times. It was often an experience: I remember goats in the aisles, rabbits underneath my seat, a piglet in the arms of the boy next to me, chicken wings beating against my head. The buses were usually crowded, and I sometimes had small children sitting on my lap.

Tacos

I forget the important buildings in Mexico City, but I remember where to get the best tacos. There is one street where dozens of taco stands exist within a few blocks. It is a classic free-enterprise situation: vigorous competition producing low prices and high quality. The tacos sold on this street are better and more varied than those to be found elsewhere. People come to this street from all over Mexico City and it is usually crowded, especially in the early evening. The tacos are all made to order. When you have worked your way to the front of the crowd and it is your turn, you call out the filling—chicken, turkey, beef, brains, *chorizo*, lamb, kid, liver, kidney—and then watch the taco-man make it with great speed. The tortillas are soft, not hard as in the United States. Most Americans have never tasted a real taco! The taco-man splashes sauce on it, rolls it up, wraps it in paper, and hands it to you. It is all done with flair. The price is low, always less than a peso. My favourite was the *taco de barbacoa*, which is roast lamb with barbecue sauce. I remember that it was especially delicious at one stand. If I were to fly to Mexico City tomorrow, I would probably go directly from the airport to that taco stand.

Tropics

Now I am leaning in a doorway in this tropical village, watching the afternoon thundershower beat down on the palms and the tropical vegetation. I have been here for ten minutes, released from my activity by the sudden downpour. I see a pig in the bushes across the way, foraging for food, oblivious to the rain. The pigs in this village wander about and eat almost everything. The roast pork must be delicious. Above the pig is a mango tree, heavy with fruit. This part of Mexico, like others I have seen, is as tropical and beautiful as anything the South Pacific has to offer. The rain begins to let up. A teenage girl walks by, too wet to care about the rain, her bare feet splashing on the muddy path. I see that her soaked blouse is clinging nicely to her breasts.

Village

Do not stay too long if you choose to live in a Mexican village. It is a matter of diminishing returns. The optimum length of residence is usually less than three months. After that the lack of stimulation becomes a real problem. That is why a Mexican village is a good place to finish up a project, but not to begin one. An American must have work to do in Mexico, and maintain a discipline. It is not enough to be just an artist or writer: you must have multiple interests and activities. It is a long day in a Mexican village. You will work hard and do a number of things and relax and talk with friends and still have several hours left over. A box of books from the United States is an absolute necessity.

Village

There was already an enormous cultural gulf between myself and the people in the village, but I did what I could to minimize it. I learned Spanish well enough to carry on a conversation. I conformed with the Mexican social customs and rules of decorum. I always used the elaborate Spanish manners. I usually looked as though I were a student living on a subsistence income: this helped, for it minimized the economic difference. I did nothing to threaten the cultural and social values of the Mexicans in any way. I treated everyone with courtesy and respect, which is very easy to do, for it seems to be built into the Spanish language. After a while the word gets around the village: he is all right. Once I overheard two people in the market talking about me. It was gratifying to hear the word *simpático*.

Village Walks

I looked at the new *tortilladora* that the women are all talking about. The owner was there, happy and beaming, a successful Mexican entrepreneur. He is very proud of his new tortilla machine, and he knows it is going to make him rich. It is new, and it squeeks, and it is funny-looking, but it steadily produces 4,000 tortillas per hour....The village

milkman, his burro loaded with sacks of milk. . . .
I looked in the open window of the candle-maker's
shop and watched the oldest daughter making
candles. The method they use is an iron ring, six
feet in diameter, with about fifty candles hanging
from it. We talked a little, she used *tu* with me for
the first time. . . . A little boy came by with a tray
of that caramel-flavoured candy on his head. . . . A
policeman was standing at the main intersection.
In a Mexican village a policeman is often cheaper
and less trouble than a traffic signal. . . . The
window of the local photographer: portraits of
Mexican children, dressed in Sunday clothes,
holding large crucifixes and trying to look devout.
. . . I leaned in the open doorway of the carpenter's
shop and watched him finish up a coffin. Good
smell of wood shavings and pine boards. . . . An
Indian woman sitting in a doorway, nursing her
child: common sight in Mexico. . . . I watched the
arrival of an ancient second-class bus, filled with
campesinos coming to market, sacks of foodstuffs
tied on the roof. . . . A baby burro! . . . Outside
the market I bought a glass of fresh-squeezed
orange juice. . . . The fat priest walked by. . . . A
mechanic was repairing a hole in a bus tire.
In the USA the tire would have been thrown away.
. . . Walked past a *cantina*, heard the lively music
from within, smelled the odour of *pulque*. . . . I
watched a sidewalk vendor doing a brisk business
with a wind-up toy. Indians from the hills stopped
and gaped. I imagined the scene in an outlying
village, when a wife finds that a precious peso
was spent on a frivolous toy instead of an essential.
. . . A man walked by, carrying a small pine coffin

66

on his shoulder. . . . I stopped to watch two masons, father and son, working on a wall. . . . Around the corner came a slow-moving group from the *carcel*, shepherded by a policeman, back from a day of labour repairing the streets. . . . Shopgirl sweeping the sidewalk with a broom. . . . I walked past the school and heard children singing from within. I stopped and listened for a few minutes. . . . Picked up a copy of the Laredo *Times*, had a nice exchange with the newsdealer. . . . I walked past the *panadería* and smelled the aroma of baking bread. . . . Watched a man paste up a *futbol* poster, then read it. . . . I saw that barber walking to set up shop near the market, in the shade under a tree. He carried a folding chair under one arm, a valise in the other. Everything he needs is in the valise. I was reminded of the elaborate barbershops in the USA. . . . Girl braiding the hair of her younger sister. . . . Four o'clock in the afternoon, opening time at the *cine*, and as usual there is a long line. The young people of the village love their *cine*: it is one of their main contacts with the outside world. . . . Two burros loaded with firewood. . . . I passed the doctor's daughter outside the *banco*. We exchange smiles and hellos now. I waited for her to give the greeting first, and then said the same: she knows what is most appropriate. This time it was *buenas tardes*. . . . Picked up my mail at the Post Office, headed for the plaza. . . .

Aidan Higgins

DISTANT FIGURES

DISTANT FIGURES

I AM three years old. Here someone guides my hand. It writes out 'I AM DAИ'

I am Dan. The same big hairless humourless hand holding a dessert spoon brings a spoonful of porridge to my mouth. I have a small mouth, a little swallow. I am hungry. I taste a warm effusion of oatmeal porridge, creamy milk, demerara sugar. It all dissolves in my stomach. The days are often cold. It's winter. In the mornings the kitchen is cold. Mrs Henry is our cook. The wood-chips catch fire in the range and the coal takes and flames roar up the flue. Sometimes the edge of the spoon cuts my lip. My mouth is too small for the dessert spoon. The spoon touches the edge of the plate so that no milk will drop onto the cloth, the table, and then conveys it to my mouth. The porridge plate has a thick edge. On the bottom it has a design. As the porridge sinks the picture appears. Always the same picture. The same pair. He: thin and fleeing. She: fat and following. Sometimes I am fooled. (My ears are frozen, I am too eager to eat and must wait for the dipping spoon, checked by the big hairless hand.) I think then that it's the wrong picture or the wrong plate, as the old picture appears under the porridge but set at a different angle, more acute or more inverted: thin and affrighted Jack Spratt forever chased by his fat and furious wife.

The hand that carries the spoon to my mouth belongs to Gina Green. "Unless you eat," she tells me, "you will end up looking like Jack Spratt." I do not wish to look like Jack Spratt.

The hand that helps me to write Dan is the hand of Gina Green. Gina Green lives in Dromore West. Gina is not her real name. I cannot say her real name. She is my nurse and Wally's. Wally is my older brother. He can feed himself. I am sweet on Gina Green.

Time passes in Dromore West. The wind from the Atlantic rattles the windows. The Atlantic is an ocean. Gina Green teaches me. With my small uncertain hand I write out at her bidding. "The cat jumped from under the bed and bit me." Gina Green corrects what I write.

I write: "I can swim like a fish in the sea." I write on a fresh page: "The man was smoking on the beach."

What beach?

Bundoran? Gina takes us to Bundoran beach.

She does not take off her clothes or go swmimming. She walks in an abstracted way by the water's edge. I am afraid of the sea and its smells. It smells of hugeness and dark green seaweed and lostness. Before it I am nothing. I watch Gina Green.

The Bowsy Murray wears a butcher's apron tied at the back. It is stained with blood and reaches to his ankles. He is a stubby little man. He stirs the tea that old Mrs Henry pours for him, drains it into his saucer, lowers his head, slurps it up. He wipes his drooping moustache with one finger and fetches up a sigh. He is as fond of his tea as I am of my porridge. His fingers are stained with blood. The Bowsy works for Young, the butcher, as slaughterman and delivery boy. He delivers our Sunday roast, a side of prime beef wrapped in blood-soaked brown paper. On his stout legs are leather gaiters; he wears top boots with iron-bound toes; his hand and clothes smell of old dried blood. His cap, which he crushes up and puts into his pocket, smells of sweat. Wally says: "The Bowsy Murray stinks."

Gina Green says: "You must not say that of a poor working man." Gina teaches us our manners. My father says: "The Bowsy Murray is depend-able." My mother says: "I think the world of the Bowsy." A two-pint milkjug smashes on the flagstones of the kitchen, splattering Bowsy's leather gaiters. He leaves the kitchen without a word. In a fit of rage I have pushed over the long table. Old Mrs Henry says: "Yule cotch it hot young fellow-my-lad when yewer Doddy hurs of duss, I'm tellin yew." "That temper of yours will get you into trouble," my mother says. They keep silent before my father and I am not punished.

I want to run away from home. I hide behind the mangle where the cats make their stinks. My mother tells me I am a bad boy. She sets penalties. I cannot escape. I do not love my mother any more.

The coal fire is burning in the range. Old Mrs Henry is roasting rabbits in the oven. I like roasted rabbit filled with breadcrumbs. Old Mrs Henry is my pal. She has a mole on her right cheek with one dark hair sticking out of it. Her hair is grey, worn in a bun. She has a funny way of talking. She comes from Omagh.

Time passes. I am six years old. I write out: "A man saw another man drowning." And: "The fat cowboy breaks stones in the mountains." And: "The cowboy was shot and they put him in the grave."

The Bowsy Murray is the fat cowboy breaking stones in the mountains. The sweat runs off him; he stinks as usual—dried blood, fresh sweat. Old dried sweat and old dried blood, the smell of leather, cloth, tobacco. The smell of an old man.

His life is not easy. He kills cows and pigs, cuts them up, delivers the parts. My father puts his best suit in the oven to air it. The little black kitten creeps in, the oven door is closed, someone takes it out in the morning stiff as a board. I weep for the little black kitten. Out motoring my father runs over a cat. Its guts stick to the road. Someone has chalked there from ditch to ditch: "O'Duffy is your man." Our car is a Coatalen-Hillman with spoke wheels and solid tires.

My brother Wally is a good boy. He does what he is told. He is two years older than I. I do not do what I am told. I wet my bed. It's evening; I'm hungry. I do not like Dublin, the distant city. I like Sligo, and do not ever want to leave my home. I love my mother and my father. I love old Mrs Henry, and the Bowsy Murray too, but only sometimes. I write: "The giant heard the boy laughing in the mountains." And: "The sun comes up with colours and the man wakes up." I write: "The giant had a tiny hand and he passed me."

We eat fish on Friday. We are Catholics. The Protestants do not eat fish on a Friday or go to mass on Sunday; they have a different church, a different bell, and they look different to Catholics. The Bowsy Murray blesses himself before he eats or drinks. Old Mrs Henry says the rosary with the maid Anny in the kitchen. Bowsy Murray and old Mrs Henry and Anny are Catholics. I write: "My name is Dan Ruttle." And:

> Dan Ruttle,
> 1 Wine Street,
> Sligo,
> Ireland.

We live in Sligo, but I was born in Dromore West. Sligo is a grey town and a fast river flows through it, the river Garavogue. We go on holidays to Bundoran and Mulranny. In the dining-room of the Great Southern Hotel I see the Bogey Man sitting with his keeper at a table near a long window. The Bogey Man is eating prunes. He is dark brown all over, his shoulders are hunched up and I cannot see his face properly, which is just as well. The Bogey Man lives in our cellar

75

with the arrow heads and the wine bottles and the spider webs, and he puts the fear of God into little boys. Into me. His keeper watches him. He is slurping up the prune juice. I watch the heavy shoulders of the Bogey Man moving, spooning prune juice into himself. The Bogey Man who lives in our cellar only comes out to get disobedient little brats such as myself. My mother tells me that I am a bold boy and that she has a good mind to put the Bogey Man onto me, and will indeed unless I improve my manners. "Flighty," my mother says, looking away and clicking her teeth; "he's flighty." My father's dander is up; his blue eyes are blazing; he pushes me in the back. "Get into the house," he says, "you little pup."

Little grains of sand fall into the stream that flows into the sea at Bundoran. Gina Green is collecting mussels on the breakwater. I am alone. The wind is blowing off the Atlantic. I am cold. A dark muffled-up figure is walking alone along the shore. The tails of his greatcoat whip in the wind; he has a big hat. My heart stops beating in my chest. The Bogey Man is coming for me. I sink down into the sand as he approaches. He comes to the stream. For me it is wide; for him nothing. Without breaking his stride he jumps the stream. I see dark eyes looking at me from under the brim of the tall hat. He makes as if to stop, but then moves on. I watch him go out of sight. Little grains of sand collapse into the stream and are whirled away. My heart begins to beat again.

My mother swims in the sea in a striped costume that opens down the back to her dark trunks.

Her back is white. I do not like to see my mother in a costume that shows so much of her back. She wears a Chinese kimono and likes to swim before breakfast. My father does not swim. He likes to drink in the bar and play golf with his cronies. His cronies are Arthur Murrable, Stan de Lack, Willie Prendergast.

I write: "A man saw another man drowning." My mother's name is Dilly Ruttle. Her brother's name is Aubrey Orr. He lives in Dublin in digs with Brinsley MacNamara who writes poetry.

> *Her shoulders shone*
> *As though polished by the admiration*
> *of a thousand eyes . . .*

Aubrey wants to be a detective. He wears rubber soles and follows people about the streets of Dublin. My mother reads to Wally and I. She reads 'Wanted: a detective, to arrest the course of time.' I fall into a ditch full of water. It's winter. The air is cold and the water colder than the air. I feel miserable as I run home.

The nun has a red face. She comes from Dingle and has a rough temper to go with the red face. When she is in good humour she tells us stories of West Kerry and her youth. She sucks lozenges to keep her breath sweet. Her temper is not very sweet. The strap lies in the shallow drawer of her desk. The desk is mounted on a little wooden rostrum. When we do not know our Catechism the nun stands behind us and pulls our ears. The nun drags at Colfer's ears as though she intended to

77

pull them off. "Will I get the strap out? Will I now?" she asks, her colour rising. Colfer's face is a curious colour, his ear blazing red. The nun drags at Colfer's ears.

"Oh you numbskull you, Colfer!" the nun cries. "Open those great waxy ears of yours!"

She has pets in the class. But I, who am bad at Irish, am not one of her pets. "Now you, Ruttle, do you know your lesson today?" I feel her standing close to me, her dander rising. "Dan Ruttle, you have me heart-scalded," she says.

She sighs, sucking a spearmint. Two desks in front of me Colfer is bowed over the desk. The nun has taken the strap to Colfer. His ears are red and stick out like jug handles. The nun uses the strap on Dickie Hart and then it's my turn.

Our desks are scored with marks from pencils and penknives. We dip our penny pens into the ink. The ink has a queer smell. A bottle of Quink is kept in the closet. The nun tells us in a resigned voice that we are without exception the most backward and lazy class she has ever tried to teach and that she would prefer to be doing something useful, like digging drains or tarring roads. She is wasting her time trying to teach us, for we are unteachable.

Sister Rumold tells us of Michael Collins walking into Dublin Castle with a briefcase gripped in his hand and marked OHMS. Michael Collins is a martyr of the Rebellion. A basin of blood stands in the girls' cloakroom and those who have had teeth pulled are going home early. I watch Molly Cushen. She is deathly pale, her face framed by long coal-black hair, and she holds a blood-

78

soaked handkerchief to her mouth. Her eyes are like sloe-berries. Her voice is deep, a strange voice for a girl. She walks over the bridge.

The wind blows in my face. I smell the river. The days pass. I walk to school. "Tussa, tussa!" Sister Rumold says, pointing with a stick. "Gradigy suss, a hain-a-dough! Gradigy suss, gradigy suss, a hain-a-dough!" as we stamp around the classroom, raising dust. Colfer is coughing, I smell his jammy breath on my neck. "Gradigy, gradigy, gradigy!" Sister Rumold intones. She stands at the door of the emptying classroom, beating time, looking amiable, repeating "Gradigy, gradigy." We march out into the open air.

With plasticine and patience, using the end of a match and a nail-file to shape the figures, my brother Wally makes a Robinson Crusoe, a little white-bearded figure with a face burnt the colour of terracotta by the fierce island sun. He is all hair and beard, with a home-made hairy hat and a parrot sitting on his shoulder, a fowling piece in one hand and a great furled umbrella at his knee. Crusoe is like Wally, who has neither friends nor confidants, none but his dumb friends. At one time he had sixteen cats; they bred and went wild, had to be shot like hares. He talks to no-one, no-one knows him. Wally is Crusoe all over again. His nature is secretive and close. He hoards things.

My father asks me: "Did you never see a crow flying and a cat sitting on its tail?" It's a riddle. "No," I say, wondering how this could be so. "Well, then," my father says. On a blank page of my sketch-book he draws a crow flying, turns over the

79

page and draws a cat, all whiskers, sitting on its own tail. My father laughs. "There," he says, pointing, "there."

Through my youth a river runs, spanned by an old stone bridge, an old fort guarded by a fortress, the most important town in the whole north-west of Ireland. The river goes under the old stone bridge. It flows through the town where I was born and reared, a town first mentioned in the history books when plundered by the Men of the Creeks, the worshippers of Odin who came ashore in winged helmets from their long-boats in the first decade of the ninth century. There stand the ruins of the old fort, a fording place in the olden times, long before the telephone and the car. There I grew up.

An old reality, a recurring dream. An old stone bridge, grey houses of Sligo-town, open-window town. Old pipe-smoking men wait on the bridge, leaning against the granite parapet, spit shag tobacco juice into the fast-flowing Garavogue, lean on the bollards down on the quays. I see an acid-faced man sketching on the quays there. It's Jack Yeats, brother of the poet, son of John Butler Yeats who went over to America and never came back.

I cycle through the town. It's grey like a dream. Coming in on the Markievicz Road I float through Wine Street into Adelaide Street, then by John Street and Charles Street into Temple, and so round by Pond Street and Chapel Street into the Mall. It's my town. I hear bells chime in the cathedral. My head is full of the sound of bells as I cycle on through the little plundered town. I avoid Union Place and Wolf Tone Street because rough boys congregate in those places, waiting to throw stones.

I am on the Mall. A breeze blows off the Garavogue that drains into Lough Gill. One of my aunts lives on the Mall. She has a phenomenally high voice and keeps siphons of lemonade. I like lemonade in siphons and am her particular pet. Summer or winter she wears heavy brown clothes that give off a biscuity smell. My mother says; "The Countess of Upper Ossary!"

I am standing on the south bank of the Garavogue. It's a grey fast-flowing river. I smoke Wild Woodbines sold in packets of fives, in open cartons. The AA signpost points towards Doorly racecourse. My father backs horses. I wait at the railway station—which is also the bus depot—for the evening papers, and cycle home with the *Evening Herald* and the *Evening Mail*. My father plays golf at Strandhill. His handicap is five. He is well-liked in Sligo. I look for birds' nests in the groined roof of Sligo Abbey, destroyed in the sack of 1641.

"Are you any good in class?" my father asks me. "Do the nuns wallop you?" I tell him that one of the nuns sometimes uses the strap. I go to early mass. In winter it's dark, the lights from the candles make the church gay. The evening light shines on old Ben Bulben. I move to the National School.

"Can you box your corner?" my father asks me. "There you will be with rougher boys. Your big brother will be there." My big brother—that will-o-the-wisp. The tuppenny Catechism has a green cover and the questions are harder, the answers longer. I get the stick. My father asks: "Are the brothers hard? Do they use the stick? "Sometimes," I say. "Sometimes they do, Da." I hear myself saying it, I hear my own voice and hate it, as I hate my skin and my clothes, sometimes.

I am twelve years old and said to be a deceitful boy. Perhaps I am. I scarcely know myself. I receive Confirmation. Now I am supposed to be a strong and perfect Christian. I know otherwise. Perhaps I am a hypocrite. My name does not seem to belong to me. Dan Ruttle. The rough boys chant, pointing at me, mocking, "Dan-the-ran, the imba-Ann, the rimbo-cocktail-imba-Dan." They go "Ah, Ah, Ah," and pull faces, laughing. They sing "Dan-the-ran, the rix-sticks-Stan, the rimba-cocktail-imba-Dan!"

"Little brute," my brother says, "bloody little brute!" I have hidden under the table and bitten him like a mad dog, on the leg. His leg is bleeding. He goes hopping from the room. I taste venom in my mouth. A heavy window comes down on my hand. My father, standing above me, fears he has broken my finger. I take sops of bread in Bovril. I watch the light go over the mountains. My tears dry on my face. My brother watches me from the door. We throw darts about, tired of pegging them at the board. One goes through the joint of my thumb. Wally runs away, crying.

I am uneasy in the presence of girls. I see a real ladies' man standing by the corner of the Cease-to-do-evil. My heart is bursting as I see the girl approach him but it's me she waits on, me she runs to, me she embraces. They walk off together.

She has a red mouth and is dressed in green. "That one is a proper Hoor," my father says. At table I blush to the roots of my hair.

My best friend is Liam Meldon. His sister is Sheila Meldon. She goes to the Mercy Convent in Ballina. Thinking of her I succeed in making myself perfectly miserable.

I have bouts of piety, sometimes in the church, sometimes in the fields. I take a prayer book with me into the fields in early summer, intoxicated by the smell of the fields and the sense of growth. I kneel in prayer before a frog-infested pond. Sinking and rising with outspread arms, the frogs kick up powdery clay from the bottom of the pool. They have the arms and legs of skinny old men. Tadpoles wriggle under the frogspawn, burrowing with their heads. They eat one another. I am discovered by a red-faced labourer with scummy lips and blush right down to my boots. I pretend to be fishing without a rod. A year later his equally red-faced brother discovers me in a less edifying posture down on the grass, poring over *Lilliput*.

"It will be the size of you," my father says. "It will be about the size of you." I lean over the bridge and pretend not to see the girls who cycle through this little plundered town. Fires glow at night all along Ben Bulben. It's the gorse burning.

I walk by myself to the north of Lough Gill, a lost domain, into a region of small limestone hills and ferny glens. Demesne of Hazelwood, Lough Gill, the road to Tobernalt, Cairns Hill. I become vaguely acquainted with a girl called Jenny Kearns, a distant girl whose name sounds like the name of a hill, whose hair is the colour of autumn

83

bracken. I court her distantly. She tells me that there is a devil in the hills. He has horns and cloven feet. I half-believe her.

She sits on the parapet of the bridge, swinging her legs, staring at me. Her bicycle is propped up against the bridge wall. She watches me. "Old Nick lives up there among the ferns on Cairns Hill," she tells me. I watch her lips saying the words. She has a lazy way of speaking.

Seated in a moored and oarless boat I stare vacantly into the river, without design or purpose in my life. Anonymous fish, mostly gudgeon, come aimless as a dream up against the bulge of the boat where my hand trails in the water. My hand hardly belongs to me. It has thickened with the cold of the river. I take it out. A marine odour clings to my fingertips.

I cultivate a taste for meditation, and have come to understand that the pleasures we get from water and earth is something that continues from the far side of infancy, from the far side of a vegetable garden and an orchard. The country touches and excites me. There were days there then when I thought all life was a dream acted out beneath the sun. I walked in Slish Wood.

Girls damp after swimming exhale a fresh breath of moss, where their bodies open there. Wrapping themselves in towels they dress. The days seem without end. I go into Hazelwood after pigeons. Two big schoolgirls are swimming in Lough Gill, thinking themselves unobserved. As they are drying themselves it begins to rain. The bolder one wears teal-blue knickers. She calls out to her friend that she is wet enough; repelled and fascinated I watch them, both naked now, splashing each other and laughing. I take off my clothes and stand among the trees, watching them. They play behind the press of leaves. Their high-pitched cries disturb me. I see reality in that flickering evasive life. The rain stops and they dress and go laughing away. A nearby haycock is steaming.

The laburnum bush is burning, incandescent yellow bloom spilling over the wall. I am alone. I take off my clothes and stand among the trees. It's an aimless kind of life I lead and it seems that the thirst for what I want will never be satisfied.

The bigger girls come screaming into the Ursuline yard. I jump out from behind an archway, get a good handful of thick brown hair, and haul away. She screams into my face: I smell bread and butter, milk. It's recess. Her excitement and fear infect me. I run away.

A brazen hussy puts a thrawneen in my mouth, takes the other end in her mouth and dares me to race her to the centre. But as the gap shortens and I see her working mouth and eyes approach, I bite the thrawneen short and give her way. She is older than I and intimidates me. I do not wish to be kissed, not first by her. She works as our maid and goes with Grogan the stable-man into the hayshed. Grogan has criminal hands. He comes out looking pale. The hussy makes as if to slap my face. "Take coward's blow," she says, and her hot breath steams in the air. We stand together near the Toss Bank, and she feels nothing save

85

contempt for me. The frozen pump is trussed up with hay, like a madman's trousers.

The kitchen range is out. Old Mrs Henry has gone home. My mother is stove-blacking the stove. A lemon drink is set out to cool. It's made of granulated crystals and must be boiled first. Nullamore is empty except for my mother down in the kitchen. My father is playing golf. I go for a walk in the fields, an open countryside beneath a pink September evening, the clouds being stained a richer colour as the light fades, the miracle of that rose colour over in the sky over Knocknarae. My life is just beginning. I feel that I will live a long life, an endless life, and my mother and father too, and Nullamore will never change.

I, who am easily put down, have this girl Hazel Ward on my mind. Modest and reserved in manner, she has a Protestant complexion and lives on a big estate, where grim Protestant gardeners work. Gore-Booths and Gregories, jay birds imported from South America, an imposing house and gardens with high walls, guarded by silence, that is her place too. The texture of her skin is glazed and clouded as though her flesh was smoke-clouded, given a kind of dusk. My eyes fall to the bulge of her thigh, the bluish veins of her wrist through the vee of the glove. Her blonde hair is cut short, the same blue-green veins show at her temples and behind her knees. I imagine something venturesome in her withdrawn gaze, in as far as I dare look at her at all. I feel embarrassed because I am sitting next to her in the bus to Ballina. We do not speak. I am too timid to speak. She looks out of the window. I breathe in her scent and an aroma more positive than cosmetics. She smells of ferns. She wears a lady's wristwatch and high-heeled shoes that cause her calves to quiver as she walks. She is older than I and training to be a nurse. She is telling an old frump that she bought stockings in Dublin, describes the mesh and brand. "At Garnett's," she tells the frump, who smells of mangolds, turnips. I have seen the marks of garters on my mother's thighs but never have I seen a young one lift her skirt. I have never kissed a girl and wonder what it would be like to kiss a pretty Proddy. I hear the word "Garnett" and look at the old frump, but it's Hazel Ward's long legs with her skirt pulled up that I see. I kneel before her and kiss her odorous things, and then I am falling back as she recoils in horror, and drowning in the deepest shame. My mother's cheeks are soft and hairless and I taste face-powder when I kiss her, but to kiss a pretty one on the lips, never. Her olive skin troubles me. Her female eyes watch me in the glass. The windows of the bus are splashed with mud and grimy rain. It shakes going down the hill. The lights are shining in Bur and I hear dogs barking. I catch a moist and disturbing look from brown eyes. Shaking from side to side as though it would burst asunder the bus goes by an empty place where curlew and plover are flying over sodden fields.

Hazel Ward lives in Carney village on the road to Lissadell. Her father works for the Gore-Booths. I have never spoken polite words to this pretty Protestant girl whose solid build and colouring disturbs me so; her young skin exudes something like the dust of pollen.

I cycle on the Carney road, hoping to meet her. Once I encounter her travelling by pony-and-trap on the estate. The paths go over the grass, under the trees, following the rutted tracks of the hay-bogies. She lowers her head going under the low branches of the sycamore. Stopping before a gate, she walks the pony over the cattle-trap. When she mounts the trap from the rear it tilts up. She drives on, not using the whip, hair blowing in her face. She belongs there in the walled estate. A big house with open doors and open French windows out of which nobody comes, except once in a while a barking dog. Hazel Ward belongs there in those enclosed and forbidden estates. Sometimes on the long summer evenings I hear the distant hallooing of the grey-faced gardeners. The keepers are always on the look-out for trespassers such as I, loose on the estate. They are under strict instructions to drive the rough boys out of the woods.

We move in silence, Republican irregulars, and they too move silently behind the trees, armed with shot-guns. Basket chairs have appeared on the terrace, and a table with a white cloth and set for tea, but nobody sits there. A long white curtain uncoils from the French window and is retracted by the draught, as a maid in uniform appears with a silver tea-service on a silver tray. I go with the rough boys and prefer to think of myself as one of them, play their games, excrete on the sides of ditches, mitch from school, get the strap. We steal apples from Nulla-more orchard. My own orchard. I am one of the lads. "Would your auld fella mind?" "Say e kum an cotch us?" "Iffen," I say, "iffen." I, who have always been a dreamy, reserved, unhappy sort of boy, run with the rough lads out of the wood, pursued by the keepers.

Is that me, the Garavogue dreamer? I think not. My real life has not yet begun.

Horses come galloping out of the top field, there is a scent of valerian. It grows on a crumbling wall. A stiff wrought-iron gate creaks shut. My father stands naked in grass up to his waist, one hand up as though about to hurl a javelin.

There is an odour of horse and horse-dung, I see guts in a bucket. Wearing leather gloves and smoking a Gold Flake my mother is soberly laying out quicklime. On the rockery paths great glistening black slugs die. I go for dry kindling in Slish Wood.

"Would you fight your match?" one of the rough lads asks. My face is close to the grass. It's something I must comprehend, something essential. The rough lad is loosening his belt and letting down his braces, undoing his buttons. He squats with an expression growing on his face as though he fully intended to explode.

"Dan-the-Ran, the rix-sticks-Stan," they chant (steam rising off the river). "The imba-cocktail-rimba-Dan" (their voices soaring away with the odour of wood-smoke).

'Distant Figures' is an extract from a work in progress entitled SCENES FROM A RECEDING PAST.

Eugene Ionesco

HOW TO COOK A
HARD BOILED EGG

Translated by
Donald Watson

HOW TO COOK A HARD BOILED EGG

Ask your dairyman for an egg. Tell him to candle it to make sure it is fresh. Normally it will be a hen's egg. You can also use a duck's egg, which is bigger, usually greenish in colour, but less easy to find. You take it home with you, trying hard to keep it perfectly intact. It is advisable to prepare your hard-boiled egg in the kitchen on a stove. But take care not to place the egg straight down on the stove itself. Put it in a saucepan, having previously filled it with a sufficient quantity of water to cover the egg. For example, a cylindrical saucepan 20 centimetres in diameter and 15 centimetres high needs half a litre of water. To obtain the water you simply have to turn the tap, which is generally located over the sink. It is this saucepan containing the water in which the egg is to be immersed that you place on the stove. If the water is cold you can heat it up, once you have lit the stove. The stove is lit with the help of a match which you take from a small match-box, striking it along either of its two abrasive sides. Then you hold the match over the holes in the burner, having first turned the knob that allows the gas to pass through the pipes and reach the holes, through which it will now shoot in the form of little flames. Instead of a match you could also use a cigarette lighter, or a gas-lighter with a ferrocerium flint or an electric battery lighter. Wait until the water boils. Then immerse your egg.

Ten minutes later it can be taken out with a spoon, to avoid burning your fingers. Then, with the same purpose in mind, pass the egg under cold water from the tap. Remove the eggshell: to do this, give it a light tap with a knife or a clean teaspoon. Once the shell is cracked, lay the bludgeon down and pick off the shell neatly and delicately with your fingers. Throw the remaining pieces of the shell, which is not edible, into a rubbish bin or down the waste-disposal unit. Then place the egg in some receptacle, preferably on a plate. With the aid of a knife you can slice the egg in two, lengthways. Sprinkle some salt on it and, if you like, pour on hot butter or oil. You can also cut it across, widthways, into smaller slices, and put them in a salad. Or you can eat your egg without slicing it up. In which case, take it in your hand, raise it to your mouth without the help of a fork and munch it like an apple, after first sinking your canines and incisors into it in order to bite off a so-called mouthful (derived from 'mouth'), then a second, then a third. Normally the whole egg will have been consumed after three to six mouthfuls.

Your egg may be eaten, if so desired, without salt, butter or oil. If you want two or three eggs, you just increase the quantity accordingly. This has no effect on the time it takes to boil them providing they are cooked simultaneously. If you are boiling any liquid or preparing any sort of food (stew, pease pudding etc.), you will notice that the cooking-time varies according to the amount or density of the substance exposed to the heating process. So long as they are cooked in their shells, eggs are an exception to this rule. If they are cooked simult-aneously, the number of eggs has no effect on the cooking-time. A peculiarity not to be despised.

If in spite of every precaution the egg turns out to be rotten, throw it away. A rotten egg can be recognized by its nauseating smell, due to chemical decomposition releasing hydrogen sulfide, H_2S. In which case you can complain either directly to your shopkeeper or to an Institute of Hygiene or Department of Public Health. Their addresses can be found in the directories issued to all private telephone subscribers, or in any café or post-office.

The hard-boiled egg differs from the raw, "boiled" or soft-boiled egg by its greater density and firmness, which is due to the dehydration that results from the cooking process. In the so-called "boiled" egg the yolk remains liquid: in the hard-boiled egg the yolk and the white have "set".

While it is cooking, slight mishaps may occasio-nally occur. The shell, for example, can split open and a part, or more rarely the whole of its contents may escape into the water. Do not be alarmed, it will continue cooking outside its shell. And when finally cooked the solidified pieces can be ladled out with a spoon. Or you can put a different egg in the saucepan and go through the same procedure again.

Some writers prefer and recommend that the egg should be immersed in cold water, in which case there is less risk of the shell breaking, since it gets warm and expands more gradually. Too rapid expansion is hard to guard against, as this process is imperceptible to the naked eye.

If you immerse the egg when the water is already boiling, the total length of time needed for it to become hard is thereby reduced. Seek information as to the exact time.

A gas-cooker is not positively indispensable in the preparation of the so-called "hard-boiled" egg. You may use an open fire, a grill, a stove heated by wood, electricity or spirit etc., and even hot sand (though account must be taken of variations in the cooking-time).

An egg is nourishing, health-giving food. It is, however, not fully recommended in all cases and is sometimes strictly forbidden. Consult your doctor and follow his advice.

Robert Nye

TRUE THOMAS

TRUE THOMAS

There was once a boy called Thomas. He lived at Ercildoune, a small market town in Berwickshire. His full name was Thomas Learmont, and people say that he was born about 1225. But when he was still young something strange happened to him which made everyone forget his ordinary name and call him True Thomas, or Thomas the Rhymer. This is the story of what that strange thing was.

It started one evening in early summer. Thomas was walking home alone along the banks of a river called the Leader Water. The air was soft and sweet. Butterflies floated on the light like little commas. The hawthorn was in bloom, as white as milk. All down the hillside the breeze was writing sentences in the whin, so that it looked as if the hills were scribbled with gold, crooked golden streams running into the Leader Water, which itself ran green and blue over the chattering pebbles of its bed.

Everywhere Thomas raised his eyes was white and gold, as if the sun in its journeys round the earth had spun a web of light which glittered now between the branches of the trees. His gaze grew dazzled by it, so that he concentrated on the innocent blue of the river instead. He walked along slowly, humming to himself, wondering if he might see a good fat trout in the shadow of the bank, and catch it in his hands, and take it home to cook for his tea.

He did not see a fish but he saw a queen. Going round a bend in the Leader Water he heard music coming towards him. Thomas looked up. Riding along the bank on a horse the colour of shadows was a beautiful lady. She wore a gown of silk as green as grass. Her hair was long and golden as the whin. Her eyes reminded Thomas of violets he had once seen in a deep wood. Her neck and her forehead were as white as feathers fallen from the wings of a flying swan, but her cheeks shone like red apples.

The music was made by dozens of tiny crystal bells that gossiped on the mane of the lady's horse. The horse's bridle made a separate sound, very clear and frosty. Together the two tunes were perfect, and it seemed as though the air itself turned into music as the lady smiled.

Thomas snatched off his cap and knelt before her. She was so bonny he was sure she must be the Queen of Heaven. "Hail, Mary!" he cried. "Hail, Queen of Heaven!"

The lady shook her head gently. She dismounted from her horse. "No, Thomas," she said. "I am not the Queen of Heaven. I am the Queen of Elphame."

Thomas was frightened when he heard this. If she was not a good spirit, he thought, then she must be a bad spirit. And if she was not the Queen of Heaven then perhaps she was the Queen of Hell. As for Elphame—he had never heard of it.

"What do you want with me?" he asked boldly, though he did not feel bold.

"I want your voice," said the Queen of Elphame. "But first you must give me seven years of your life."

"My voice?" said Thomas. "How can you have that? And how can I give you seven years?"

The Queen of Elphame did not answer him. Instead she held up her right hand and waved it in the evening air. Immediately there were blue birds going round and round her wrist in a circle, a bright bracelet of birds, lovely to look at. Then she held up her left hand and waved that also. On the instant there were green birds going round and round that wrist, another bracelet, winging in the opposite direction. Thomas could not take his eyes off the two circles, the one blue, the one green, the little flickering wings, the swift bird-bracelets.

He began to feel drowsy. His head was full of the sweetness of the hawthorn blossom. Tears came to his eyes.

"Now it is time to go," said the Queen of Elphame.

She kissed the neck of the horse the colour of shadows, then she mounted it. Thomas climbed up behind her. They rode off together. Blue and green birds, shaken free from the Queen of Elphame's wrists, whirled about their heads as the horse rode over the Leader Water. Thomas thought he must be dreaming. All he could see was the white of the Queen of Elphame's neck and the gold of her streaming hair. All he could hear was the crystal music of the little bells. The horse galloped fast. The horse galloped faster. Then the horse was galloping and galloping so fast that the trees and the river, the hills and the sky became one blur, and then not even a blur.

The music of the bells was like an alphabet in another language. Green and gold, white and blue, Thomas's world spun about his head and burst in his eyes. Green, sang the bells. And white, sang the bells. And blue, sang the bells. And gold gold gold, sang the bells. These colours were all that Thomas could think.

Then the colours went out and the horse slowed down and the song of the bells grew softer and Thomas saw that they had reached the edge of a desert. Thomas had never seen a desert before, but something told him that even if he travelled the whole world over he would never again see one like this. This desert seemed to begin at the end of all he had ever known. It was perfectly flat and empty. There were no colours anywhere.

It was a place where you would meet no-one because there was no-one to meet. It was a place where you would lose your shadow if you walked there for long. It was a place where if you wrote your name in the sand it would soon disappear for ever, leaving not even a dot behind. North, south, east and west, as far as the eye could see, this terrible desert stretched. The Queen of Elphame drew rein and the horse stopped.

"Thomas," she said, "do you see the road that we must take?"

Thomas stared at the desert.

"No," he said. "I can see nothing. Only desert."

"Look more closely," said the Queen of Elphame.

Thomas rubbed his eyes. He stared at the desert, trying to make sense of it. It was then that he saw three roads. The first road ran towards the north from where they stood. It was narrow and twisty and as Thomas looked along it the way seemed dark with thorns and briars.

"What road is that?" he asked the Queen of Elphame.

"That is the road to Heaven," she answered. "It is a hard road, as you see. We shall not take it."

Thomas looked at the second road. The second road ran towards the south from where they stood. It was wide and straight and seemed to run downhill all the way through lucid fields of lilies.

"What road is that?" asked Thomas.

"That is the road to Hell," said the Queen of Elphame. "It is an easy road, as you see. We shall not take it."

Thomas looked at the third road. The third road ran towards the west from where they stood. It was narrow in some places and wide in others. There were flowers here and there beside it, but also nettles. It went up hill and down dale, and sometimes it was straight and sometimes twisty.

"What road is that?" asked Thomas.

"That is the road to Elphame," said the Queen.

"It is a hard road and an easy road, as you see. Only those who can stand still in themselves can go down it. Only those who know that they know nothing can find the way. Others may point it out, but no-one can walk it for anyone else. It is not the road of yes or no, but the road of road. And you and I must take it."

The horse the colour of shadows moved forward. Thomas and the Queen of Elphame started down the third road. On and on they went. It grew dark and then darker. There was no moon in the sky above them, and no stars shone.

Once Thomas thought he could hear the sound of something like the sea, but it was a curious inside-out kind of sound, so that instead of waves breaking on rocks it sounded more like rocks breaking on waves. After that he heard nothing: no birds, no words, no wind, no echoes; nothing. The horse's hooves made no noise at all on the road and the bells on its mane did not ring any more. Everywhere was black and silence.

At long last Thomas saw a tiny speck of light in front of them. They rode on and the speck of light grew bigger and brighter. Now it was as big as a fist, now it was as big as a man's head, now it was as big as a whole man, then it burst about them like a wave, a bright foam of light, towering and splashing, and Thomas saw that they had come out of the dark into a fine country. There were green trees and green rivers, blue hills as fat as pumpkins, valleys full of feathery blue green grass, white fountains, gold mountains, and green birds and blue birds everywhere. The crystal bells rang on the mane of the horse the colour of shadows, and its bridle chimed, and there were bells on every branch keeping time with that tossing music, and more bells bouncing on the crests of the fountains, and bells on the birds as they flew. Everything seemed to rhyme with everything else. Everywhere was light and music.

The Queen of Elphame drew rein and the horse stopped. They dismounted in a walled garden. In the garden was a maze. They walked round and round in the maze until they came to the middle. A gold tree grew there. There was one silver apple on the tree. The Queen of Elphame plucked the silver apple and handed it to Thomas.

"Eat this," she said, "and Thomas of Ercildoune will be True Thomas."

Thomas took a bite from the silver apple. "True Thomas?" he said. "What do you mean?"

The Queen of Elphame smiled and did not answer. Thomas ate the rest of the silver apple. It tasted of night and white and gold and music. It tasted of desert and bells and hawthorn blossom. It tasted of birds in a circle and all that had ever been, and was, and would be. It was an apple that gave Thomas the twisty power to speak straight in rhyme of what had not yet happened, and the hard power to foretell future events as easily as if he had already seen them pass. It was because of the powers of the silver apple that he could be known as True Thomas. The name of the apple was Truth.

When even the pips were gone the Queen of Elphame took Thomas to her glass castle. It was a shining place. The fires that burned in the grates were made of diamonds. Bright harps hung in the air and played when the Queen looked at them. The floor was paved with sunlight and instead of doors there were rainbows. Peacocks strutted up and down on the lawns outside, talking in Latin and Greek. Strange plants grew in the Queen's garden, with labels round their necks to tell you what they were called: triolets, odes, epodes, sestinas, cantos, centos, and sonnets.

The Queen's servants brought Thomas a cloak of green silk and shoes of green velvet. He lived in Elphame for seven years. The bells rang, the fountains sang, the hills stood blue and still with birds above them, and Thomas walked and talked each day with the Queen from morning to evening. She told him all sorts of secrets and instructed him in all manner of mysteries. She taught him that everything is related to everything, and that a poet is only a man like other men but more so, having the power to see likeness where others see opposites. She taught him to bind things up in words to follow the lines that linked them, to make a net like the stars in the sky, wide-meshed but letting nothing slip through. She taught him how to think in images and how to feel in words. She taught him that man is a fragment who can be a whole. She taught him that there are things which words alone can talk about, and other things which all the words in the world cannot say. The seven years passed quickly. To Thomas they seemed no longer than seven days.

At last his time was up. Thomas had to return across the blackness and the silence, along the third road through the desert, on and on until he got back to Scotland. Settled once more in the little town of Ercildoune, he never forgot his meeting with the Queen of Elphame, his journey to her strange and beautiful country, and all that he had learned there when he ate the silver apple. He wrote poems and songs, and went up and down in Scotland telling or singing them to all who would listen.

Some of his poems spoke of things that had not yet happened but which did happen while he was still living among men. Some of them told of things which did not happen for centuries to come, but when the time came they came true. There are still some left to come true.

When Thomas was an old man the Queen of Elphame came once more for him. Just as she had done before, she rode in early summer along the banks of the Leader Water on her horse the colour of shadows, the small bells making music as she came.

"Thomas," she cried, "True Thomas, my Thomas, your time has come. Not for seven years, but now for evermore you shall be mine."

Then Thomas mounted the horse the colour of shadows behind the Queen of Elphame and rode away with her. He lives in her perfect country on the far side of the desert and the silence, along the long third road that is both twisty and straight, and hard and easy, where there are green trees and green rivers, blue hills as fat as pumpkins, valleys full of feathery blue-green grass, white fountains, gold mountains, and green birds and blue birds, birds everywhere; and he lives for evermore.

Jan Quackenbush

SIMEON IN MEMORIUM

Born wild to be subdued
Born freely to be caught
I go not as I am
Knowing the difference.
What is left is yours
And was yours to begin with
And used by you as you saw fit
And that's the end of it
The first and last of it
But to understand it

SIMEON IN MEMORIUM

An Issue's Issue

Now knowing now losing conciousness body
shattered broken it is swamp covered with
mist it is jungle groping for me it is mist
circulating upward above through spaces of
spaceless mind dreams carrying me away from
edges edges and surfaces temporal and transient
it is fever charring heart and lungs the tongue
taste of blood of instinct summus of self
 Goddamn Goddamn Goddamn
 Small and world coming to an end looking
up seeing no one down and seeing the earth
the shrapnel of the mine my flesh my blood
my leg two yards away the viscera half off the
trail
 My God

Lingering   long enough to be tossed   merci-
lessly   on waves of shock   engulfing   then receding   the drowned valleys of my breathing lingering
long enough for Death to claim me as a debt   to
observe the sun hovering near noon   the jet
streams   like fresh scars   slashed across the face
of the sky   the ants digesting dried blood on
boots   their pincers soon gripping bits of sweat
glazed skin marrow bone chips with the
past more vivid than the present   which has no
future   no doubt   I see that I see that I was
once on the plain and crossing the plain   covered
with white frosted leaves whose seams had come
undone   when without questioning the fear of it
of being innocent   the first step   then
  to fall
  to become a rose in the garden of fixed prerequi-
sites
  when   as now   I lifted my eyes to my own level
  I measured the distance to travel   sensed the
infinite and still vision or imagination   the horizon
could not be seen   horizon turning on the hour
with glimpses of plain   again   forest and mountain   prismatic shade and sun   until   at last   I
was beyond and deeper into self to the end and
back again full circle   with no end in sight   and
now as then   I repeat   I cross the plain to enter
forest to climb the mountain   revolving once
more   sealing Time with hesitation   knowing
that hesitate and I   I will   see God   a God with
the art of disappearing   and I   knowing that I
shall be discovered lying here   helpless   already
dead   am gasping   in the swollen sea
  O how the mind bubbles! I dance! I leap! I

scatter the dust like a sunbeam! I soar to the highest branch! Scale all parapets!

Until a stab of pain cuts me down and I sink once more into the abyss like a deceived Italian renaissance. Perhaps in the dusk of a vaporous evening, from a Venetian canal, I am gathered in pieces by a delirious gondolier. Ah, I am mesmerized by visions, puppet with a heart! Thirsty dreams, hallucinations, all in chaotic sequence, toil and boil in the brain like raging elements in a Wizard's pot. One must settle down to die, eh Graymalkin? But how the mind rebels!

I see the afterbirth being discharged with a careful sigh, and mother, not given to overt expression, is embarrassed by the noise. The doctor is chuckling and licking my face with a sterilized cloth while the nurse who is barren is concluding as usual that emitting a child is a very extracurricular activity. Mother feigns exhaustion by allowing an arm to dangle just so as she is wheeled on a stainless steel cart to her room on another level. The Nam doctor pauses   the Vietnam dawn   the doctor pauses for coffee, and the nurse   the dawn this morning   the nurse glances at his crotch. Beneath a blue   the Vietnam dawn appeared this morning a blue blanket, I am being laid among my   like a petal   my dreams in Maternity 307   like a petal of the rose.

The dawn, yes, as red as a burgundy wine from Les Vins de Dienbienphu. I was glad to see it come, erasing as it does the phantoms of the night, but so slowly that the first scarlet rays feel as sullen and as arched as melancholy. Yet, for those of us who never beat the system and consequently find ourselves chosen to guard the camp's perimeter when the orders are posted in the Orderly Room, the calico weaving of daybreak's tapestry is spun more in the heart than in the tired, strained and half-closed eyes. The expectation of an undisturbed sleep chisels the smiles upon our fieldstone faces, not the   my hair was long and brown and not the radiant version of   and fair, wind blown of a Hollywood sunrise; the smile only large enough to   tousled hair   to hold a cigarette. I scratched the....

Hair long brown and fair, being tousled by winds in the autumn of their time. Eyes blue and dark, large with precision, curiosity, rare one-time harmony. Early morning in early September, doves flying South, I standing at the edge of the forest looking down. Seeing God. Wiggling a bare foot in damp earth, prodding God with my toes. God responding with characteristic lethargy, rubbing legs together, hopping away with a chirp. Then pulling myself together and looking up. Seeing the sun's eye slide behind a yellow thin cloud. I deciding to decide to climb the mountain.

Slight step forward to trip on stone I know is there but do not see; small wonderous body falling to ground by instinct. Resting upon the pros and cons; hours fleeing one upon another, merging within the angles of enchantment. I pulling sand, so much sand   pulling myself together, crossing the   everything blasted with sand   the idea that for the rest of my life   no firm footing ever   never will I look at God again.

...scratched the sand from my hair, my lips, the lines in my face, my ears, from inside my nose, from my collar, from the front of my sweat soaked shirt, my belt line, my fatigue pants, my green canvas boot tops, and leaned my elbows upon the sandbag bunker, my chin in my hands, holding my eyelids apart with my fingers: I could see the thin black wires stretching out to where the claymore mines perched forward on the rims of their isolated shallows like unearthed skulls. The gloved fingers of the day's first sunlight curled around the fold of night's ebony blanket, pulling it back star by star, causing pale pink sheeter of atmosphere to shimmer against the delicate blue. The mines would have to be retrieved and entombed for the day. The Officer-in-charge would examine the bunker and then   I'm five years old, but then we would be dismissed, able   the mirror   at last to sleep. The mirror's reflection   I closed my eyes and . . .

Wait   oh wait   the images   memories   cascade too fast   too fast   There is

Five but more, standing before mirror: exact duplication but for the real. Who can be me? Tilt head, even so. Cover eye, even so. Smile, frown, pretty, ugly, nice   mean   ferocious   hurt happy, even so. Yet, who can be me? Turn away, turn back, even so. I am repeated.

Where's mama, then? Hands and knees, crawling now beneath beds. Mama? Standing, running, leg eclipsing leg, feet squashing thick shag carpet, plaited rug, tumbling, stumbling, falling, up stairs, pause, turn, down stairs . . . Mama? Door . . . open! Out and out onto wide expanse of lawn! Mama! Mama!

The sense of being left behind: hiding behind

tree, staring, spinning, plain, forest, mountain, beyond and deeper into self! Car on driveway, mama leaving house and walking upon walk calling: Simeon! Simeon: I thinking she will have to find me. Smiling to self: she never can. Then noting different voice, different tone: Simeon! Simeon! I thinking perfect game here, behind tree.

She has not looked! This, too late! Run, Simeon! Chase! Fly! Fly! Mama! Mama! Fall! Pain! Yes, and, lift head, lift eyes! Tears! Tears! Yes, and, wipe eyes, tears remain. Stand, Simeon! She will come, seeing you. Lift and hold you! She always has. She always has.

Whirling back from nowhere than from fear, standing before mirror, my stare considered these things: days, nights, more than I reveal, and she has not returned. She is not repeated. I am not, even so. No one is. Yes, and I will be missed. Sudden fear being felt: if I am wanted to begin with. Instinct   weight on elbows, my eyes closed instinct Officer-in-charge before sleep instinct now as consciousness, I turning   loneliness so far away from home   turning, leaving   I closed my eyes and thought   leaving myself behind me.

  . . . thought of friends so far away, of last night's nervous sounds, of the yellow flares we lit the darkness with, of the poor emaciated dog shot and strung on the concertina wire frontier. I heard the moaning wakefulness behind me in the camp, felt the vigil at an end, could smell the thick black boiling coffee, could hear a sergeant's scowl; then an eerie demonic laugh scattered the violet impressions.

(By Hands I Hold)

Are eyes opened
    The orb standing still could be an eye
    The soft billowing surfaces could be clouds or
ants
    A grazing sound sounds like swamp grasses
sighing in what may be a breeze   Sun or moon
I cannot tell Pain sparking now and then so
alive I must imagine
    The last sharp stab of pain is retreating the
last audible breath barely traced Eyes only
a spasm can release them
    The mind climbs like a swan's white flight
eastward to the World
    I can't go home this way
    Home sinking into the dream the dream
while the blood the blood turns black There
may be a search patrol out for me   carrying a body
sack My belly is a canyon crawling with worms
I pass Blacking out Blacking out again merci-
fully slipping deeper through the last layers of
the abyss
    Darker
    Darker
    How is it I still breathe
    The body must be drained of sap by now the
brain collapsing the heart squeezed dry
    Mother you once told me that Death is the
easiest undertaking of all Now bend your tongue
across the sea and say that you were wrong

MOTHER

Once I saw the child. Or was it the sun? The moon?
Perhaps the smile in the palm of his reaching hand?
The memory is too vague to tell, but I remember
the feeling of seeing the child.

"Mama!"

The feeling itself was amazing or similar to, if
not actually the same as, that reservoir of emotion
which cracks my eyes after I have

"Mama"!

had to stop again and gaze at a picture of my youth.
I: splendidly courageous, daring the world to
cancel my existence. Today I won't invite the
world to watch me move unless things are properly
arranged beforehand. I

"Mama!"

will never allow myself to be interrupted again.
It would be like going bald! Although I do find
it increasingly difficult to control invasions now.

"Mama!"

Or was the feeling more akin to pity? In the
sense that I, when an old woman, will cross to my
window and, standing alone, look into my garden,
see how the roses have withered, and say: Pity.
How beautiful it was.

Simeon, I suspect, is different. It's difficult to
think of him without realizing the extent of his
youth.

"Mama!"

He doesn't seem to be afraid of noticing the differences among things. My own fears are reserved
for unseen things; things which as they are, I
never see.

118

"Mama!"

Perhaps this is one reason why Simeon is distant from me now. He seems to be so certain of what he sees! Rarely will he respond to my affection. I, well, he is a hostile child. I certainly never considered feeding him from my breast!

"Mama!"

Perhaps, then, it should have been said thusly: Once I felt the child! Or, now you judge for yourself, was it the sun? The moon? The smile in the palm of his reaching hand? Indeed, the memory is too vague, but this I *am* certain of: the feeling frightened me. It is conceivable that Simeon felt likewise. It might have been the only instance of "rapport" that we ever established between us. I don't believe that we share anything

"Mama!"

now.

No, not that feeling of remorse or whatever, but something quite different frightened me. Was it the child I felt or something else? An obstruction? Even the labour, the burden, the weight, the eternal waiting for! is part of the mystery. I am like an old woman who simply cannot remember much of what she had! Well, but birth is such a conundrum. I only remember the feeling of feeling something. Now, I am between whatever it was and nothing. This is the sensation that I fear today. It torments me! It cannot be exactly analyzed. And really, I doubt that I am capable of seeing how the roses have withered. I am turned from the inside out, you know. I will never say: Pity. How beautiful it was. I will never want to!

"Mama!"

I cannot answer him. What does he see? Nothing could be further from the truth than Simeon. He is sensitive beyond his right to be so. He is irritating; for like a sparrow, were it caught in my house, I cannot easily pass his existence up for nothing.

"Mama!"

Well, but he's died you say. And in battle, too. In that ugly little war. Then I must think of him, him, what, as if in the past? I can't imagine his being in combat to begin with! Simeon considered himself to be a poet, you know. Of sorts.

"Mama! Mama!"

Well. His father put an end to that.

FATHER

For all of him, whatever he was, he was not unique as children go. A single concept of Time, restoring the chaos in a dream, is not sufficient to say: I alone have dreamed this. All children dream, yet how many pursue their dreams? I can tell as well as you, but do you think they number a crowd? Can you say without once looking down that we share the view? What is left behind is before us yet to step upon.

The dream is yours or mine, but not ours together. The moment of dreaming is what we would share, if anything. I would sometimes say to him: You are Simeon as I am I, and for both of us, whatever our mettle, we are not unique. We alone do not dream, although we dream alone.

Like any man, I have wandered between my own misgivings, yielding to laws that I would never condone. Shielding depressions born from ignorance, bending as any tree must bend before the onslaught of seasons, I gave much of myself to Simeon, being sympathetic to his process. I believe he knew, or sensed, the turmoil in this house. My wife was careless, and although anxious to please, recoiled in the face of failure. We had too many wasted moments, and, eventually, we parted.

This was not unseen by Simeon, whose eyes were larger than the deep. He found corners and shadows more comforting than chandeliers, and was unlike my other children in that respect. Oh well yes, yes: once the days were happy days; were gathering crowns of dandelions. Full of Simeon standing behind the hickory tree as, for him, floating God's eye's clouds blinked and three o'clock shadows were angels to play with. And the tree was not an old tree or wicked, and Simeon would stand there were the grass lifted up to it, nudging the roots, and looking into mysteries as if spellbound. Such as these were days of open eyes and tumblings, and we were well set in wealth. I could afford to tolerate. But Simeon shook the roots of things, and I warned that one day the leaves would bury him.

I wanted him to grow and mature like a stalk of wheat. I think education comes in many ways. School is important, of course. Military service. Now there's a real catalyst! I wanted Simeon to be poured into the broth and stirred with the other ingredients of manly experience. I thought of him emerging like a synthetic diamond. He needed to have his poetic elbows rubbed by the raw and the real. I sent him to college to become a doctor or accountant; to mould him into a useful citizen! Well, it wasn't long before he became influenced by the so-called intellectuals, and worried himself about philosophies, politics, even moralities. Then he decided to become a poet, and boy did I pull the rug out from under him. I refused to finance that kind of attitude, and when he had to quit the college the draft board picked him up. You know, children squirm like fish caught in nets, and are made better by it!

SIMEON

I   child   walking   alone   how long I to continue
I to where what I is there
   Plain   Forest   Mountain
   Revolve heart   holding Eternity's marred jewel
losing radiance
   Sound I sound what I hear   as you imagine
   See I see what I see   as you believe
   Age   and the present will not last   regardless
of the need
   All won lost or free
   Walking now through fields of clover   paths foot
printed by morning cows   Birds rising   darting
through air   and I wishing I were there asking
later what kind of birds these are   someone will say
swallows   someone will say sparrows   someone
will ask me how they turn   I will say they turn
like goldfish turning forever in a glass   They fall
like acorns falling forever for I wait forever for their
falling   I will say they rise like leaves rising forever
as they do   forever

Then one will say nothing   one will say sparrows
and one will ask their colour   The colour of   I
will say   the river   The colour I will of my   say
hair   Then two will say nothing and one will ask
their size   That of my eye   will I say   Then
three will say nothing   and yet   yet I'll still
not know the kind of birds these are

Green edge of plain
A miracle of morning
Rising grey mist
I come to you entering
Accept me
Raise me gently upon your wings
Circulating soul of life
I am nineteen years into you
And what dream is this

Flowers   I went to you for my nurse was very
kind   She held me to her kisses   telling me stories
to laugh of things I knew   pretending to be
surprised   She told me letters and numbers and
words   I will always want to hear her voice which
never shouted in anger

Flowers   I wanted to ask her where my mother
had gone

Flowers   I wanted to ask her where my father
was

She would say nothing until I had run into the
fields for you for her for I had watched her gathering you for herself   forever

Flowers   I had many things to ask   but one by
one everyone was silent   It was better   when I
did not ask a thing   when one by one everyone
would tell me more than I knew from the sun to
the moon When the sun hiding behind what hill

was time to eat before the moon was time to sleep
I sleeping   then   with nothing to ask

Imagining you now everything within you red of
all purple in all blue of all yellow green   you
flowers   are   everything   forever

I would have given you to my nurse like evening
Evening chasing evening's men to surround them
For I had watched her giving you to herself in
evening

With smiling
And with whispers of a Spanish rainbow
But I was holding hands held

(Mind Whispers)

Walk it smooth   Walk it smooth   Walk it
smooth   Walk it smooth   Simeon get your
dead ass up!
Recalling light of dawn ascending   timid heart
courage reveals But Sarge! I just got off guard!
Then to embrace the field   pierce forest edge
discover ravine That don't mean shit to me,
soldier! The man says we is going out! Light
brightening valley of lake shore cottage
window That's all I know! I don't know you is
tired or feeling bad! Eyes to lay upon gently as
if to tell a secret   Light of day Or got a itch or
hung up! Just like I don't know Jody! absorbed
perceived   comprehended as mind whispers
and Or It's snowing in Alaska! Now what I say?
I say move your ass! dream shadows hide
body intuits awakens into day Why are we
going out? Jesus Christ! We just got off a patrol!

Robins in tree squirrel approaches nest a
sudden fury And besides, I get time off for being
on guard! Footsteps below in last year's pattern
the year before Look, mutter, don't go asking me
or telling me shit! That's an order! Father has
returned Comfortable knowledge that But
not alone.
You wanna court martial? You wanna disobey
my order?
No Who is she father's new wife My new
mother But yes and Hey, man. Like you're
really hyper this morning! Come on, Sarge, who
is she Eyes of stone Her voice loud like
thunder on the lake We've been busting ass in
the boonies too long to play REMF games.
Today I shall go into the woods again Sensing
the freedom there Tell it like it is!
Sensing there of what is there
Goddamn right the ole ass-kicking Sarge is
hyper this morning! Light of day descends
Night and I staring at stars divining You
know what's happening, baby? We is crossing
into Cambodia! The lucidity of corporeal enti-
ties The depth of perception We is getting
inside a whole new fucking ballgame! assisted
by pure white celestial diamonds polished by
the moon What?
This one more thought of youth overwhelm-
ed Diamonds lost
What I say?
Now are simply stars Soul being sensed with
religious clarity Look, man. I only got three
more months over here! I'm short!
persuades

This kid ain't going into no Cambodia. I'm going R & R to Vung Tau! i exist everywhere in all things i am harmony i am tranquility Simeon, you is so wrong your eyes is crossed. You going on patrol. i lie upon my back feeling myself slide in the spectacle of galaxies What about Marchetti? He's still in the hospital! Mystery of Universe unfolding in my eyes my heart i am yes and Roger that, blue eyes. And you is covering his place for him! Embraced am i by light of transcendence The moon's eye my eye Now I know you're lying. Nobody walks point except him.

of vision medallion of my mind. But that that that could could Where we got him. And we don't. Does we.

The thin vague veil of sadness which perplexes me Cloud So that means somebody else gotta point, don't it. Like I say. demanding my attention gathering all the meaning I attach to it That somebody else is you! Man, so quit with that cat-eye look. as it advances across the sky above the lake until the stars It ain't my doings! I didn't spread no word to hump it in Cambodia! until all moon might disappear forever Sudden violent anger I didn't order us on a Recon patrol, or you to go guard either! recalled at the prospect of the cloud's intrusion Dig it? This Sarge ain't no Lifer, man. No way! Recalling how I sat up as the cloud edged nearer to the moon The man says it to me to lay his word down, so what I say? I shouted at it I shook my fist at it Stood and cursed it I say one more time. Get your ass out and your

gear together! Pleaded and then commanded
it to disappear
We is moving one more time. And, Simeon,
you're too short to die.

Voice echoing across the darkening lake until at
last the sky was utterly devoid of light   until I
felt the harsh sting of tears burning my   cheeks
with a flame that terrified me   until I could make
no sound   but was caught in the throes of un-
controllable sobbing as I clasped my hands around
my knees and held them tightly against the pain in
my chest while tears ran streaming from eyes
which sought only beauty and poured upon a chest
which yearned only to ache from the vast pounding
of a heart in happiness and I carried out in a world
whose forces were beyond my understanding
despite my comprehension
All was fixed in suspension until a rough
muscular arm wrapped around my bare shoulders
another curled beneath my knees and I was lifted
to my father's heart with a tenderness I had
forgotten long ago
His face brushed against my own
Whisperings were heard
I was carried back into the house just as lightning
split the sky   as thunder roared across the universe   as rain raped the lake

Pause   Simeon   Reflect   Simeon

Nature is closing to the night
Her silent suspecting orphans are nowhere
sheltered from the storm as they wait   expecting
like lavender skies

And I   slipping out   submitting   dreaming disengaging myself

From myself

As imagination strains to perceive new forms of being   a   new   soul   painted   with   the   harvest juice of my own earthly reality like a landscape of autumn's day-long evening

A new face   body and mind   the infant seed

A capsule protecting the prospect of desperate growth

Of enough time to germinate

Of   enough   time   to   transpire   the   tragedies perceived

(HALCYON)

turning   head turning

　　　　neck muscles throbbing   turning head to ease pain   mouth sealed by dried blood lungs closing   sucking air   air slanting in through nose   perhaps through chest

　　　　evidence of rain   perhaps rivulets of sweat body sap   O DEATH

Time   Time   Time

no sound   no recognition of sound   no arriving patrol searching for Pfc   to fill body sack   to place in soil back home

enough   enough   enough

losing consciousness.

```
i i i i i i i i i i i i i i i
 i i i i i i i i i i i i i i
  i i i i i i i i i i i i i
   i i i i i i i i i i i i i
    i i i i i i i i i i i i
    i i  i i  i i  i i  i i  i
   i i i i i i i i i i i i
  i i i i i i i i i i i i
 i i i i i i i i i i i i i
i i i i i i i i i i i i i  you
 i i you i i i you i you i you you
you you you you you you you you you you you
```

Sunday morning, spring, you are at the seashore. You climb to the top of a small cliff and see a kingfisher being swept along the rocks below, its wings beating against the gale. Just when it seems inevitable that it should crash against the stones, something occurs which causes the bird to soar upward on the invisible currents of air to a turn and a glide beyond danger. Seathed by the sunrise, the kingfisher weaves a darting pattern across the outstretched sea where everything appears tranquil and safe, only to return with incredible speed, time after time, headlong towards the rocks. This, without apparent reason, until at last the kingfisher crashes and falls alone and dead.

It is as if expected to be but to watch silently the ebb and the flow the mystery of suspension fills you with the thought that there is an emptiness in the manner of many events which you cannot explain   You feel the wind many times over   You turn away and yet   like a season in the air   you turn into....

Ann Quin

EYES THAT WATCH
BEHIND THE WIND

EYES THAT WATCH BEHIND THE WIND

What was happening?
She no longer knew. Feeling only her pain. And
his. The weight.
   Pulse in the stone
wanting to hear it. See it. Not enclosed. But see
and hear it emerge from the skin. Transparent.
For the touch. Like the necklace of delicate pink
shells round her, hanging over one breast. But
even these she knew would break soon enough.
She liked holding them, one by one. The smell
of sea This naked back caught by light. Ocean
reflected. Mountains of waves rolled them together,
separated them on to the beach. Breaking out of the
sand he had been buried under. Her own burial
with the branches, twigs he had put in, without

her knowing. When opening her eyes she saw arrows pierced into her body under the sand mount.

The memory of this
and the wreath of white flowers high on some rocks facing the ocean, she had suddenly seen one morning, after sheltering in a cave. A cave she had left quickly because of two fishermen who leered at her from some rocks nearby.

They had been in Mexico nearly three months. Moved into, out of three places. Yet she had no sense of placement with him. For him. There had been once, but that was hard to recall. And if remembered only fell heavily between them.

A longing
for rain. Heavy rain through the night. They were told it was the rainy season. The days continued hot, dusty, oppressive. Mountains seemed to be pushing their way nearer. On being pushed by thick white clouds clinging there. The only clouds.

On their way to Cuetzalan, south of Mexico City, they had passed the cone shaped volcano Popocatepetl contemplating Ixtaccihuatl, the White Woman. Snow covered belly and thighs. The outlines of these volcanoes were not visible. Sometimes even their heads disappeared, then reappeared, risen islands floating high above them, where stars must have been, and clouds formed smoke columns above the snow.

Ixtaccihuatl
Popocatepetl watching
watching behind the wind eruptions under skin.

Under eyes. Of those who wore slick neat city suits, who stepped heavily along the hot concrete. She was glad to leave that.

Glad not to be furtively looked at by those dark shells.

Eyes never meeting her own.

Glad she would perhaps no longer hear the word 'Gringos' shouted out. Or be spat at by passing drunks. Clutched by beggars. Stoned by boys. Be confronted by huddled shanties in front of middle-class apartment boxes. Confronted by her own strangeness, helplessness in the face of their defeat, their resigned acceptance of life conquered by death. The family of God knows how many living in cramped quarters, who smiled cheerfully at her. The girl of nineteen who had just given birth to her third child. She found it hard to smile, feeling self-conscious of her clothes, the difference in their lives. The simplicity yet hardness of theirs. The complexity and softness of her own.

They arrived in Cuetzalan, a town appearing to be from another century. High up in the mountains, where walking through clouds seemed more than a possibility. A place once invaded by the French, driven out by the Totanaca Indians. She liked it, admired at once their dignity, openness. Their immaculate white clothes. Women in long skirts, brightly embroidered sashes, lace blouses, purple, green yarns of wool twisted into their dark hair, piled high on top of their heads. Some carried babies on their backs, in baskets of string woven onto wood, supported by a strap around their foreheads. Yes, she felt self-conscious, conspicuous in her short dress, and they were curious, but they nodded, smiled, spoke gently: *Adios Adios. Buenos Dias. Buenas Noches.* The soft padding of the men's sandalled feet. The firm tread of the women's naked feet.

Part of the earth.

They at least had accepted, made use of the land. Had no use for, no need to fill in the Void like the Mexicans did with noise. The sound of radios. Music relayed from a gramophone through a loudspeaker in the belfry tower, that started at 6 a.m. every day, and continued most afternoons. The town had, in fact, only had electricity for a year. The Mexicans loved their new toy. A television set was a proud possession.

Once, going for a walk along one of the many stony tracks, passed by white clad Indians bent double with their load of sugar cane, following their mules also laden with cane, or long heavy planks of wood, she heard from a wooden shack the sounds of Louis Armstrong. Again a loss of placement. The sound reminding her, taking her back. Forward. The knowledge that soon she would cross the border to a country, his country America, where once more she would feel a stranger.

And England?

How distant it seemed now. Yet in moments a longing.

But for what?

She had no sense of belonging there either. A vague feeling of 'roots'. A certain kind of identity. The freedom of knowing her way around. But the greyness. Oh that grey, grey thing creeping from the sky, smoke, buildings, into the pores of skin. Grey faces. No she could not go back to that.

And here
well here there was a stillness, a gradual regaining from the landscape. The maize as tall as trees. Bananas unripe, and oranges. Coffee plantations surrounded by mountains, layers of deep blue fading into clouds, mist. Shrillness of insects. Locusts. A startling brightness from the poinsettia, flowers of Christmas Eve, above her head bent low. Now high, watching the turkey buzzards circle, in their search for snakes. Then down at the line of leaf-cutter ants coming and going. Armies of them. A moving line of leaves, twigs along the track, up over the rocks into a small dark hole.

Up the mountain into a cave.
The sense of this land, a kind of timelessness caught her often by the throat. The line at the top of her shoulder blades crossing the spine. The tension there.

Expectation of his touch.
The placing of his tongue, razor sharp. Could enter. Squaring her for that, feet together, head neither too high nor too low. To make the last pass of any series of passes in silence. To perform some act that would provide an emotional yet rational climax.

She tried fighting off the longings, demands for what had been. Tried moving with the Mexican sense of no midday. No evening.

En la Manana, en la tarde, en la noche.
Even in this 'out of the century' town she felt

weighed down by some slow stirring thing. The very earth. Smell of hard dry cracked earth. Sweat. Urine. Heavy scent of flowers mixed with smoke from the factory where sugar cane was melted down. Smell of dry blood. Pigs slaughtered. Shrieking of a pig escaping, caught, pulled by a rope, tethered to a rock, still shrieking. How could people live with this, under it, under the midday heat beginning so early in the morning, without it all thrusting through, quickening the pulse like the hump of muscle rising from the neck of a fighting bull, which erects when the bull is angry. How could it not all make the hands quick to grasp the *machete* from the leather sheaf hanging always close, so close to a man's body. And strike. Slice through another's skin?

Mass in the morning. Massacre in the afternoon. The ritual. The exorcism. Hadn't she been all too aware of this at the first bull fight? The heavy wary, sometimes dazed bulls. The swift agility of the matadors. One or more unarmed with a cape, but carrying the banderillas, provoking a series of charges; running in zig-zags, or seeing how close they could approach the bull while playing, without provoking a charge. The banderillas discreetly decorated with coloured streamers, that looked like flowers. More and more of these soon sticking out of the bull. From under these streams of blood, mixed with sweat. Continual prancing, or rigidness yet fluid dance, of the matador in his skin-tight pants, heavily brocaded cape. Light-hearted airs, graces, smiling forcedly. Flowery style, lengthy repertoire, until finally she found

herself also taken in by it all. Admiring the redondo
of man and bull executing a complete circle. The
decorative pass with the cape in which it was held
by one extremity, swung so that it described a
circle around the man. She almost forgot her
earlier nausea at the matador's arrogance, his
Hollywood smile. While the bull paused, blinded
by dust, sun, blood. And panic. The *olés* of the
crowd, or their hissing when a picador missed the
bull when charging, and the point of the pic
slipped over the bull's hide without tearing it.

The waiting of a picador, waiting for the bull to
get close enough so he could place the pic properly,
but the bull struck the solid wall of the mattress
covering chest, right flank and belly of the picador's
blindfolded horse. The horns going under, again
and again, until man and horse toppled over with
a thud. She had looked away then, choking back the
vomit, not wanting the others, the Americans,
she sat with, to know that she was 'chickening'
out. When she looked up again to the dragging
out of the horse by a trio of mules, she noticed
several people's faces quite pale. She glanced at
him, crouched forward. Yes, he could accept this.
This death ritual.
The meeting place of challenge.
It was absolute. It was in silence. Especially the
final act, as the matador furled the muleta, sighting
along the sword, so that it formed a continuous line
with his face and arm preparatory to the killing.
The two facing each other. It was physical. Sensual
almost. Yes, she could understand his fascination
with a sensual kind of violence. Seeing it there in

his face, watching intently every move man and bull made.

The pulse in his neck moved
a small creature, ready to jump out, seize her own neck that arched back, down, where she felt the ache. The ache at times of wanting this violence in him to break out. Devour her. Hurt me hurt me hurt me. But not in this way. Not in the heavy silence of them both facing each other, weapons concealed. The final turning away, not even in anger, but resentment.

The challenge not met.
At such time she almost wanted the frenzied shouts of an audience: *Anda*—Go on

Anda

Anda

Anda

Not this rejection.
She couldn't take it. Nor the verbal attacks. When words became only accusations slung at each other. If no words, then it was a sword-thrust that goes in on the bias so that the point of the sword comes out through the skin of the bull's flank.

The man did not go in straight at the moment of killing. She remembered vividly the six out of eight bulls suffering this prolonged death. Haemorrhage from the mouth. Not just one sword, but several having been badly placed, and entered the lungs. Neither did she want the sense of triumph. The *vuelta al ruedo*. The tour of the ring made by the matador who had killed perfectly.

But anything
anything rather than the silent anger hanging heavily like the afternoon heat, when even the

sheets were a a weight on her limbs. And the angles of his body jutted out—thick branches thrusting her to the edge of the bed. Her own arms crossed over, around her neck. Breasts.

The weight
a stone tied to an inside cord in her belly, turned, turned and twisted. The thud thud thudding of her heart. Reminding her of the Indians in New Mexico. Their drum beats. The pulse quickening, or slowing down accordingly.

Asking
Praying
Asking
The asking
the praying for rain. Touch of his hands. A lightness. Fingers in her hair. Fireflies coming in through the open shutters. Then the longer hold of his tongue in her. Her mouth on him. Tongue resting there. A way of knowing him. He had been unsure then. Not sure what she wanted. Needed. Thinking perhaps she had dozed off. Or had passed into one of her trances. Towards those trances he felt a kind of envy, a fear. Could not share. The body removed. That she had gone far out. Into some area he could not be placed in, or find a place there with her. But he had his own areas. His own crablike places. Once they had watched whole colonies of crabs down over the rocks. Cancer. His sign. He was fascinated. She was curious. What parallels could she perhaps discover? They seemed to move slowly, but in fact moved quickly. In order to move forward they had to move backwards.

It was precisely this movement that often startled her. The way he had of carrying the weight of the past. In himself. To himself. In moments she accepted. But resented the way he tossed his head, stomped off, without a word, into his studio. She had the feeling he dived in there as he had into the huge waves. Waves she was for the first time in her life frightened of. So she would remain, alone, on the beach, under the shaded thatched covering, waiting. Watching. And he'd emerge, flushed, triumphant. Not like now when that transparent quality of skin from water had some-how given way to a paleness, as if pressed down under many stones. Or covered by sand. But his eyes, mouth had been left uncovered in the burial. And when he had heaped the sand over her, patted it down around her neck, he left her head, face uncovered. The trance then had been quick in coming. She had nearly reached some point in space. A space in herself, yet outside her body, when she felt his mouth, warm, salty from sweat, sea, on her eyes. She was jerked out of an area into a place she did not recognize, and then she saw the arrows. Breaking out from these she ran.

Screaming silently
in a space she had so nearly found, but then filled in by the arrow points. She threw her body, no longer her own body it seemed, but just a body hurled out of the ground, into the mountains of water, she bent her head under, rose up, bent again, and struggled out. Further out to higher and higher mountains. Away from the beach, where she knew he waited, watching, not quite knowing. Unsure again.

And if she returned?

If she chose not to, but moved on out into the ocean until perhaps the area she had so nearly reached could be touched upon.

Later when they touched, it was as if someone else touched her. She gave herself up to this. From out of the past, with lovers she would not see again, be committed to. It was new. The lovemaking. Slower. Sensual. Longer. Backwards. Forwards. Sideways. She no longer placed herself over cliff edges. Under water. In space. In every room of wherever they might be. On the floor. Ceiling. Walls. There was at least no longer that need then. Everything was there. In many ways strange. Liking it. But questioning it later. Wanting something else. So when he made movements for her tongue to move in the way he wanted. Knew. The way that gave him pleasure. She still held onto him in stillness.

A resting place.

This way of holding him, as if she would never let go, perhaps swallow him whole, made him question. Made for movements that did not measure her own. Made her draw away. He grew small. Limp. She stiffened, layers of skin beneath froze, then started shaking. He got up. A dark shape against the window. She knew he could see the palm trees circling the square. Leaves quivering, fan like. The bells started ringing. Soon the music came. Loud. Sounding like a funeral march. Something like Elgar. And even before the sun was up she heard the voices of the Totanacs setting up their stalls under the kite-like awnings.

143

After breakfast, exhausted, they went down into the market. Wandered past those who had perhaps walked from villages many miles away, taking two or three days, laden with wares they hoped to bargain over. Sashes. Shawls. Vegetables. Fruit. Pyramids of oranges. They pushed through the crowds, down the white stone steps, to where a large circle gathered round a 'rainmaker'. In front of him were bottles of liquid, in which appeared to be floating various kinds of twigs, or pieces of bark. Also spread out were large coloured pictures of diseased bodies. One in black and white of a nude woman clutched by a skeleton death figure, behind her, with arms outstretched as if ready to devour her also, a masked surgeon. Meanwhile the 'rainmaker' thumped his chest, shouting to the silent, watchful Indians, that his 'medicine' could cure cancer, bellyache, headaches, and alcoholism. He had a small *machete*, which he used with dramatic gestures, pointing at the pictures, the various diseased parts, then bringing the *machete* up, making a slicing gesture a few inches from his naked sweating chest, while his eyes rolled white. The performance must have lasted an hour. She watched the Indians, who intently watched, listened. Finally when the 'rainmaker' stopped shouting, held the bottles up, many of the Indians passed their five *pesos* over for the 'medicine'. She wondered if he sold 'love' potions.

They walked on through the crowded streets, past stalls with many coloured ribbons, material. They were stared at. Surrounded when they decided to have their feet measured for sandals. The leather felt good, strong, yet light on her feet. But she was aware the women giggled as she walked by. Back in the hotel she took the sandals off. Soon she heard the priest's voice, as if through a microphone, sounding similar to the 'rainmaker's'.

He had gone across to his studio, opposite the hotel. A large empty loft place he had rented with much haggling from a man whose face was covered in carbunkles. Who always sat outside the doorway. Was his body covered in carbunkles? She shivered. Yet it was hot. Unbearably so. She found a shaded part on the balcony to read. Even reading proved difficult. She found herself looking down at those who came and went, or just squatted outside stores. Beggars who stood silently outside the hotel entrance, and waited until someone from the kitchen brought them something, a *tortilla*, something perhaps they themselves had left at lunchtime. Beggars that were very different from those in the cities. Their eyes alone asking, without demanding.

She looked across to where he sat, she could just see his hands moving forward, backwards over paper. If only. If he would lean more forward. Look up. Out of the window. Come to her now. She looked further down and watched the carpenter opposite, always at work. Painting bright blue coffins with white intricate designs. Small coffins. Sometimes larger. Often he carried one down the street, on his back, supported by the strap around his forehead. At that moment he was carefully painting black shiny crosses, very large, like bedposts. Suddenly she was aware of someone standing behind her. She knew it could not be.... she would have recognized his steps. It was the boy who cleaned their room. She smiled, then turned away. He came nearer, leaned on the table. She quickly picked up the book and pretended to read. She knew he watched her, watched without focusing his eyes on her. As if in some trance. He was so close now she could smell his sweat. What did he want? She did not know the Spanish even to say please go, please leave me alone. Did she want to be alone? She was alone. And the boy who cleaned their room, in silence, every day, who slept in a dark alcove downstairs, she felt his loneliness. He leaned nearer. Breathing heavily. She stood up, called out to him across the street. He came to the studio window, she gestured frantically. He shouted to the boy to leave. The boy left muttering *'Gringos Gringos'*.

She went into the room. Lay down. Music. Bells. The priest's voice, or was it the 'rainmaker's' again? Continual hammering of the carpenter. She went out to the balcony and looked over the railings at the huge wooden Quetzal birds. Dozens of them, with white painted eyes. Beaks ready to erect. She walked along to the small chapel, she had not somehow dared to enter before. Confronted again by the Quetzal birds, a dozen at least here faced the altar. Next to the altar a wash basin. She left quickly. And went for a walk. Men stared, whistled, shouted out. Ah, how different when walking with him. She climbed over some rocks, through some maize and crouched in an alcove of orange trees. Remaining there until the sun went down behind the purple, blue mountains, outlined against the sky. Frozen waves. If only it would rain tonight. She walked back, eyes lowered. As the Indian women, the older ones, lowered theirs. And the men leaned against white walls, seeming to laugh. At her. At death, somehow depriving it of any power to wound. A detachment from life. From death.

She remembered one of the many legends about the volcaneos:

Ixtaccihuatl was a lovely princess wooed by Popocatepetl. When he failed to win her, he turned her to stone, and then himself too, so that he might contemplate her forever.

Ixtaccihuatl, the sleeping princess.

As she walked down towards the hotel she heard distant thunder. Wind out of the dust from the high plateau. Through the maize stalks. Perhaps it would rain at last. At last

Rain.

The water-carrier passed her. She could never quite decide whether or not he was a half-wit, or just very drunk on *pulque*. He paused, tossed his head, laughing, and came towards her. The buckets tilted on the pole, water spilling out. She nodded, and walked quickly on. She hoped he would be back in their room, wondering where she had gone. Worried perhaps. At times in the heat of the afternoon she felt almost an urge to go out alone, walk into some part of the jungle, amongst the palm trees, bananas, maize. Give herself to some Indian. Without words. Be ravished. Even raped. Then killed. A quick death from a *machete*.

The violence of that afternoon sun. At least now there was the wind sweeping across from the mountains, through the valleys. Stronger. And the thunder nearer. She had a headache. Felt a cat-like restlessness.

He was in the room. Brushing his hair. He did not say anything. But continued brushing, brushing, brushing his hair. She longed for a touch. A word. Something. Later as they lay in bed, she leaned over him. The rain started. Soon heavy rain like tidal waves on the roofs. She took him in her mouth. He moved gently, then faster.

Rain above. Below.

Soon rushing down her throat. Filling her. Filling the area she had so nearly reached.

So it was in moments.

The next day again began with loud music. Bells. The carpenter hammering. Road menders just outside the hotel. The breaking of stones. Two men sifted limestone. Stones laid in a mosaic pattern. They all stopped working as a pig got loose again, was lassoed, led down the street, squealing, struggling back from the rope.

Soon they would leave this town. They had decided. She had decided. He accepted. She would go on ahead. Alone. To New Mexico. He would perhaps join her later. A temporary break. A rest. From the pain that still lingered. The prong of a harpoon catching under the skin. And what would happen, or not happen, she accepted.

She would wait.

But not a waiting between life and death. Arrows and stones. Rather a sitting still on some high rock facing the mesas. So still she would seem a statue. And the lock would be part of her weight. A part of his. A place where they could contemplate each other. From a distance. An area they could meet in. Separate.

Touch in silence.

Nicholas Rawson

JULY'S FOUR

JULY'S FOUR

I

*As if when on a winter's night
you sit feasting . . . . a single
sparrow should fly swiftly into
the hall, and coming in at one
door, instantly fly out through another.*

THE DEALER ACKNOWLEDGES HIS SOURCE★

Chant (passerine)

★*Bede : Eccl . Hist . ii . ch . 13.*

Pass
passereau
ach Spatz
sparrow
sparred
within
sparsed
sparsim
it passes
so
a ditty and
a

                          sparrow
through the barn or hall Why
lines of a tale long told told
well before my time selves here
kings transient pretend pretence
towards mere speech from a throne
of bales the distant motor race
some dog's caught bark scarce
fox or in the still sounds
musical from a box secluded
lovers in broad vista of
champaign call pastoral the
tractor's near loose rattle
real in a field & brief a

                          sparrow
through the barn perspective
eight miles to the rise July
drone on old English summer's
rule who knows an hour a day
dulled year insane not all so long
but seems too long too short

in turns yet all a noon & all
remain

                all permanent
How alter gossamer sweep vague
on fields the winging dove
sheared sheep's slow move & pause
fenced cattle stockstill in the eye
this far from vantage scan
again the twitching tail for
image haze of gadfly circle
black white head & haunch

Pass
passereau
&c.

Termed this first part beneath
the hanging corrugated tin
in sun dulled rust above
old blue & vault of all
past present hours & days
whole human bestiary
entire the hours the hours
love life love & death
Who cares
no philistine so much
as hides inside my maze

II

                    The sparrow's
brevity (now gone) to dance
in haste the forecourt grass &
dung accepts my own how slight
is all become how passing slight
these echoes of old song I'd
have a spirit in the land sure
pray to it all else ephemera
my common tone why still this
questing for some end scanned pause
how state the songs have sung
too long street ballads fade
another day who would not weep
not whine his while some grief
with lute to play or smile

                              & know
that crater such a scene
conceals heigh-ho the no
things o my misters all
how jingles jangle jar old
youth lies yawning after
joy pleasaunce grown ancient doth
all cloy some other barn some
wheres a time beyond the
pastoral
too far

                              too far
sure now too far away to
catch love limbs' lazy tangle
thighs with arms writhe to

wrangle flesh in soft sperms
easy mingle roll in hay call
it summer jay & magpie flash
the meadow croak cry brittle
harsh the dull wives' warnings
lie a

                                                sparrow
steps & scratches on the tin
above thin dusts from perished
mortar time slide down dried
runnels These fond too fond
descriptions false framed pictures
lapsed the cattle slow recede
from sight seen sex machined &
dead

Chatter copulate o copulate
sharp thorn dry rasp quick thrust
or two till jellied in the skin
Fatten populate
o populate
till puffed my world did spin
in peril at the whirl

                                        At sea
four mariners silent on a
deck becalmed kept watch
swift instant of that swell
& felt as fishing men wild
spasms of an earth spun mad
apocalypse my dearest friend
is procreation of one being for
end

in that time which it is
indoors it is indeed not
touched by the fury of the
winter but yet.

Two men lolled in a room
behind a banquet spread
close told of splendours they
had seen once spent whilst

intermittently

a serving girl removed
their bowls & bread
refilled this ceremony
held in war shrill pipe
of shells high overhead
replaced with more
the ravage of the pair dull
maudlin drunk recapped
the yore days' usual toll
as each by turn took off
his several articles of
martial role till stripped
to mask expressionless & raw
one fat as commerce
his other thin as law both
ceased to muse in silence
odd to note while all this
time the girl came in & out
attired each trip
once more with what
they did by turn again

discard
white ashes in the grate
burnt out

Part purpose of this mime
enclosed for July four
within the barn where
sparrows pass shows proof
enough a literary goal
though too long ill this
tale's inheritor with his
infection from a time now
cold

'Shall I at least set my lands in order?'

Shall I
shall I

pause deadstill
the figure waxen
froze enframed

Shall I accept as starting point
or aim from which this aging
figure first did work in recompense
vieux style by newer name collate
that mess called cultural cut clear
the patterns of an end in
subsidence of mud foundations
primal crumble slide their
never less *but yet*

Pass
passereau
&c.

Come go
go to it
smiling
friend & folly
go by return

SOUVENIRS

Seven fish
Mouth to tail circle chase
The brass plate centred with
A sun ship seven waves still
Copper sea Winslow at the Bell
A sometime paradise of peace
To catch the voice high
Hesitant or wise or both
How tell or why no elegy
His bow slight incline
Cocked old head & white
Fair host reception ever
Noble to my friend I spoke
Thick in the chairs brown walls
& floor quick voices in the
Corridor no call there ever
To participate sure honour
Seldom held yet well content
To know them dull & bright
The mouth to tail round chase
Smooth sun ship on the seven waves
Symbols none arcane I would
They were but cool attendant
As some interlude before the

Journey down the avenue
Long Stowe's unmeaning every
Where presents

then incantate

or

FOUR JINGLES & ANOTHER
PAUSE

The grey rook up & flies away
Dung flies feed on dung
Swarm from dung & come
To fasten on the dung

A sparrow through the barn
Winter winter side to side
Fly fleet an hour all time
For all the us brief gadfly day
All the us by turn to play

Quick count the old man's sweep
His scythe's past measurement
The old fool's no younger
Should he make his sweep narrower

Come come does it matter (does it)
Thunder rolls on lands gone grey
All the us in turn to pay
The white rook up & flies away
Caw caw the frost is come

fare well rook
fare you very well

III

AN OFFICIAL COMMENT

Her eyes & lights
pierce the night mile straight
silent soft susurrus back
old home old bed & older yet
old hope daft dream the dark
all gone long vision of the sea
chase sun ship seven static
waves however anchor even
in these days for pause but
sailing on old dutchman selves
false images harsh rent behind
drawn curtains velvet torn a

this smallest space of
calmness being passed
almost in a flash from winter
into winter again,
it is lost to your eyes.

sparrow's
excrement yet wet vague flutter
in the rafters heard the wings
begin the flight across the warmth

to end where they began the
windows gape thin panes
cracked in the storm & hail
winter to winter come too quick
fled the in-between too late

HER FRIEND COMMENTS

Still here together in the
hall arms head coats
all damp quick fear to grip
as one we grasp the moment
taut the wings the wings begin
last journey through the room
which those before old friends
termed journey of the soul
by night across the sea
some more or less I'll term
it too this time again since
when the flight begins I am
already happy at its end

FINAL COMMENT OF AN ELDER
FROM MAENTWROG

                            Once
he said deep hid in rhododendrons
ferned edge still Llyn Hafod Llyn
the Lake of summer dead association
an intense regret suffused my being.

entire of course he said that
instant with binoculars when loomed
each petal's vast lipped bloom
enlarged & burst within my head
the lake glass shimmered undulating
lines between the boughs all dark
around & softly lapped I *saw*
(he writhed in shadow on the bed)—(the Denbeig-
                                      shire Infirmary)

no doubt he said the sex of God
I was vouchsafed you understand
an image too immense which drags
me to my present life its *slow*
encroaching end such piss too often
cause for plaint & wild lament
he said adjusting voice precise
to murmur twice

   too often cause for plaint
   & wild lament

Shortly after preparation for sleep
he sings

Pass
passereau
&c.

IV

   Somewhat like this
   appears the life of

164

man : but of what
follows or what went
before we are utterly
ignorant.

PERHAPS THE FRIENDS
CONVERSE

did you hear it did you
really listen quickly in
the rafters tell me did
you tell me please we're
not one I know it only
else we hear it all
together flying there
across the beams in the
shadows warmth & sunlight
did you hear it do you
please say you do say
you heard them wings
from winter winter fleeing
does it matter will it
ever wish you'd hear it
say you heard it like my
mother told me once said
it flies across the rafters
from a window to another
winter winter through the
room then you know she told
me all ways *see* it right
from start to end sure she
said that tell me quickly
did you hear it do you

truly in the rafters flight
in shadow through the room

HER FRIEND IS SILENT

"Such" he said, "O king,
seems to me the present
life..."

Who told her mother
same as the other
she told her daughter
so did her mother

so I tell you